The Head and Not The Heart

by
Natalie Keller Reinert

The Head and Not The Heart

Copyright © 2011 Natalie Keller Reinert

ISBN: 1466291141

ISBN-13: 978-1466291140

For Cory -
You believed in me.

Acknowledgements

To my Retired Racehorse readers,
who always urged me on...

And to my childhood trainers, who taught me how to sit a
horse, and occasionally threw me over one...

And to my parents, who supported the whole madness:

Thank you.

The Head and Not The Heart

One
Last horse of the day

I relaxed in the saddle, loosening my joints, in a bid to keep Saltpeter quiet, and tried to enjoy the morning. It was a show-stopper, as usual, all fog winding through the branches of live oaks, an orange disc of sun visible faintly through the opaque gray, just lifting above the rolling horizon, the damp air carrying the sounds of whinnies and neighs from a thousand horses in the fields around of a hundred farms. Oh, winter mornings in Ocala are spectacular. They stretch on and on, the sun coming up late, past seven thirty, when exercise riders and gallop girls like myself have already put in half a day's work.

We'd galloped a mile and when I turned back to see the horses behind me, I could see the steam was rising off their hot, sweaty backs and necks. My grandmother, never a romantic, once said steaming racehorses looked as if they had the devil in them. I'd been five when I found a book of slick black and white racing photos at the library, and brought it eagerly to show her while she sat studying her Bible. My grandmother had been overly interested in the devil.

We must have looked like that picture now, and I couldn't have denied Nanna at that moment if she'd risen from the grave and proclaimed every horse there to be possessed by a demon. There were five other horses in this set of advanced youngsters, five other leggy two-year-olds, blowing out their nostrils and snorting at the shadows and the imagined tigers in the bushes, lurking on either side of the gravel pathway back to the barns, lusting noisily for hot young racehorse flesh. Sitting upon them, bodies moving easily with their curvettes and feints, five other riders, identical in our polo shirts and safety vests and hard hats, identical in the whips in the small of our backs, shoved unused through a belt loop, identical in our hard-set jaws and wary eyes.

Luckily our expressions and posture were as far as the resemblances went, and I meant to keep it that way. They were hard men, older than me, and had spent their lives in this outdoor life, with faces like cracked, forgotten leather parching in the afternoon sun. I moisturized and sunblocked frantically, but there was no keeping at bay the Florida sun, and no disguising those little squinting wrinkles next to my eyes.

Saltpeter was the last ride of the morning for me, and his gray hair was all over my black polo shirt. I tried to brush it off and found that the shirt was damp with the fog. The droplets of cloud were slowly sinking through, and I suddenly felt chilled in the cool morning. There's a moment when all the heat of exertion from galloping the horse gives way to the cold air outside your skin. It feels like sudden-onset hypothermia. But here we were back at the barn, and it was time for a hoodie for me and a knit sheet for the horse. We rode into the open shedrow and I ducked under the doorway as Saltpeter turned of his own accord into his stall. I gave the big gray horse a pat on the neck, nodded to the waiting groom who stood with a leather halter and shank over his arm, and started to dismount. From behind me I heard a noise in the shedrow which gave me another chill, raising goosebumps on my bare arms, unrelated to the weather.

"Horse!" someone shouted frantically, and I saw a blur rushing past the open stall front, big and dark and fast. Saltpeter flung up his head and I caught desperately at the reins, the thick rubber slipping through my grasp. The colt darted forward through his open door, chasing the runaway, and, half-off already, feet clear of the stirrup irons, I went off backwards and hit the ground hard, grunting as I lost the air in my lungs. My head snapped back and my hard hat thudded against the concrete wall.

Just another morning.

The grooms were shouting, chasing the horses, which was nonsensical, because nothing will make a terrified horse run away faster and farther than a shouting person running after them—they find it hard to differentiate between mountain lions and humans sometimes, and I imagine that I would too if I had evolved with my sole chance of survival in the world being a keen sense of hearing and scent, and four very swift hooves to gallop away on. Through half-closed eyes I watched them, and when the tall Englishman who had been watching the horses work turned back to look at me, I waved an arm at him to go on after the horse. I was pleased that he'd thought of me, but I was fine, just winded. And the horse would always have to come first.

That's just how we live.

I closed my eyes and listened to the melee as if detached from it all. What a life, I thought. What a life I lead. Another morning up at four thirty, another morning spent in boots and kevlar vest and hard hat, whip in hand, wrestling and shouting with barely-two-year-old Thoroughbreds, practically wild frontier mustangs in their feral flight reaction to every object or surprise that came their way—stray candy wrappers, stray leaves, stray cows, other horses, probably even their own mothers. Another morning getting dumped—and how typical that it would be the last horse, the last ride, the last dismount, when you think you've gotten through the day unscathed. Another bruised rear end to favor. Another dented hard hat to discard.

What a life, I thought. What a life I lead.

The fog was finally lifting when they came back, leading the two shame-faced horses, who both looked completely winded and sore after their excursion. I could see them through the stall door; I still hadn't moved. I was too busy grousing, too busy feeling sorry for myself, too busy questioning all my life's decisions. This is the sort of thing that happens when you get up too early, get dumped off a horse, and haven't had coffee yet: you start remembering that you had a 3.8 GPA in high school, and that office jobs, complete with padded desk chairs and climate-control, don't start until nine a.m.

"Up the driveway, on the pavement, right up to the gate, and a huge bloody dent in the iron gate where someone slid into it. There are scrape marks for fifteen feet across the bricks," Alexander reported in haughty disgust, his British accent particularly pronounced and betraying his bad temper. He came into the stall where I sat, arms over knees, still in the straw where I'd landed. "And what the hell are you still doing down? Do you need an ambulance?" He didn't look alarmed. Either he knew that I was in a foul mood, or he really didn't care that I could've been hurt by such a silly fall.

"I'm fine," I grumbled, and put my hand up for a lift. He reached out and pulled me roughly to my feet, then pulled me up against him for a brief kiss.

"Silly girl," he murmured. "Who falls off the last horse in the last set in the stable? Only you."

"You may laugh," I said stiffly. I couldn't laugh about my riding with him; he was the only person on earth with whom I was insecure about my horsemanship. "But my ass is not laughing. My ass is ready for a feather pillow for once instead of this hard ground." I toddled away from him, tossing my whip to the nearest groom, who snatched it out of the air and grinned laughingly at me. Speaking no English, his toothy smile was thrown to me like a bone to a dog; it was the closest he'd come to supporting me against Alexander, who would cheerfully work me as hard as he did the barn crew, and wonder if I didn't thank him for the privilege. Hell, sometimes I did. Protégé to a great conditioner, with a born and bred eye for a good horse—a dream come true, of course. Depending on your dream. I was starting to question mine. I brushed my hand thoughtfully across the seat of my jeans, dislodging the pebbles and mud, and thought of a bath and a book. The sort of things normal people, who didn't run 200-horse farms, got to do when they hurt themselves.

"You fell in the *straw,*" my lover and boss said from behind me, completely unsympathetic. He steered me away from the golf cart and back into the barn. "We better watch those horses walk out."

The shedrow had been raked smooth already. Some silly groom had stayed behind and groomed it into a perfect tranquility garden, as if we were done for the morning, while the two miscreants were out being chased down by the rest of the barn crew. The hot two-year-olds, Saltpeter and his delinquent buddy, a bay simply called

Max, were being led through the grooved lines of sand while the over-eager groom leaned against his rake and shook his head in despair at his own foolishness.

Alexander stood still in the center entrance, watching them walk away from him down the row, kneeling down in the dirt to get a close look at the way their ankles and hocks and knees flowed and clicked, and shading his eyes against the emerging sun's rays to see if the hindquarters moved evenly, or if one slouched lower than the other. I watched him, and then the horse, trying to see what he saw, and when Saltpeter went on a second pass, I closed my eyes against what I suspected.

Just then, Alexander turned to me. Bad timing; he didn't tolerate sentimentality, or hiding from the facts. The heart has no place in the horse business; he had schooled me on my first day. In this business, you think with the head and not the heart. "Open your eyes, girl," he fumed. "Did you see it?"

I nodded. "I saw it."

And I had: an ever-so-slight catch in the motion of the left hind ankle, an arrest of motion before the true depth of the ligaments was reached, a tiny shortening of stride. An injury.

He stood up and watched the horse amble away from us before turning to disappear around the corner on yet another circuit of the barn. "The left ankle," he murmured. "There'll be an almighty swelling in it this afternoon. If that's all." He turned around and shouted down the shedrow. "Hey, Manuel!"

A small man appeared in the doorway of a stall, past a bright-eyed horse pulling hay from its net. He climbed under the rubber stall guard and set his pitchfork against the wall before regarding us silently. He's thinking that his lunch has just been cancelled, I thought. And he's right. Poor guy. Horses pay no attention to anyone's schedules but their own.

Alexander barked out instructions for cold-hosing and bute in the horse's lunchtime grain, which Manuel presumably understood, because he nodded and said, *"Si,"* which is about the most reaction I have ever gotten from him. One of the morning riders had been a groom once, but he was a nice guy and I found it hard to imagine him being as taciturn and silent as our training barn crew was. One certainly never got the impression that they loved horses. And this was very hard work to do if you weren't doing it for love. Very hard. I rubbed at my backside again, feeling the bruise and wincing. I must have hit the concrete berm which ran around the inside of the stall, to support the clay foundation of the floor. Naturally, to fall in a stall filled with straw, I'd hit the concrete. I didn't usually think too much about tumbles, but this fall offended me more than most. I had started wondering what these mornings were all about, honestly.

Alexander asked Manuel again if he understood. The groom, who had lived in America for seven years, understood perfectly. He nodded sullenly and went on. A good lunch break and nap, spoiled. Because Alexander had hung around the barn and his stupid girlfriend couldn't sit a horse. Oh, I knew what he was thinking. It was what all grooms thought, and I had once been one. But you cannot deny good horsemanship. Give the man his due—Alexander put his horses first.

We made our way back out to the golf cart. I slid into the driver's seat cock-eyed, favoring my bruise. Alexander settled down in the passenger seat, sliding aside a sales catalog with a cover photo of a foal peering through its mother's tail, meant to entice even the most hard-hearted horseplayers that the time was ripe to purchase an in-foal mare so that its get could eat its way through your savings and break your heart, and he sat contentedly, waiting, as always, for me to drive him. "Shall we go up to look at the yearlings now?" The morning routine, first the training barn, then check in with the yearlings, and with the broodmares and their foals. I just wanted to go back to bed.

I took off on the gravel drive, and the cart whined and rattled its way past the training barns, and up the hillside.

Two
Horse country mornings

There is nearly always a fog in these winter mornings, and if you live in the right sections of Marion County, the expensive, limestone-rich swaths of countryside where the live oaks have been growing for hundreds of years, their Spanish moss dripping down over the stable roofs, then the mist twining through the trees, the five-board wooden fences, and the shadowy figures of horses, at grass, or jogging on the track, or being led, hot and steamy, in bored circles after a workout, is simply too beautiful to believe. Saratoga has her summer-green elm trees, but our ancient live oaks are pretty spectacular in their own right, and they have leaves all winter, unlike some northern trees I could mention.

Cotswold Farms was scooped out of a valley in one of these sections, in the rolling hills of a village called Reddick, just north of Ocala proper. Village is a misnomer; it was really a collection of horse farms with a gas station at one of the rural intersections. Our training track was the centerpiece, located deep in a valley, adjacent to the long shedrows of the training barn, with the green hills above it peppered with barns and horses of all ages. The broodmare barn. The weanling barn. The yearling barn. The breeding shed. The stallion barn. And close behind it, riding a high slope and nestled within a grove of oak trees, the house.

Down here in the valley—and please note that I'm talking about hills, here, not mountains like northerners or people from out west might be thinking—down here in the valley is where I have spent my mornings for the past five years, galloping on the track, schooling babies at the starting gate, teaching galloping youngsters to skip to their other lead on the turns, and then riding them back into the training barn, under the overhang of the shedrow, where horses poke out their noses over their stall screens to greet their friends, and hand off my steaming wet horse to a groom so that I can go get on another one.

The middays, and the afternoons, I spent at the top of the hill, running the breeding operation. I spent spring and summer in the broodmare barn, more often than not, gossiping and learning all that I could from the vets that came in their dually pick-ups, rattling with stainless steel surgical equipment, cabinets chock full of hormones and antibiotics, and bearing strange scandalous soap opera stories from the weirdest place a person could ever live: a racehorse town. I spent fall and early winter in the yearling barn, where the weaned foals, who had spent their summers by their mother's sides in the fields, were brought in to learn to live as adult horses, with stalls and schedules and halters and humans, and along with the grooms I was pummeled and bitten and dragged by the adolescent miscreants that we would name yearlings on New Year's Day. In the blinding-white barns, with their wide, airy shedrows like the porches of a plantation house, I was the authority, the queen of the property.

In the house, I would always be less so. I might talk to the vet myself and bring the information back to Alexander for him to digest, but my personal opinion wasn't really in play. My veterinary opinion, in fact, wasn't very often solicited or appreciated at all. I was a young female person, raised in America on show horses, and therefore a corrupt presence in his insular world of men—British, one would hope—who cut their teeth on National Hunt horses and marathon-galloping hurdlers, the likes of which we Americans could never hope to ride or breed. Their soundness legendary, their miraculous winning streaks in the face of years of strenuous racing legion, they compared in no way to the toothpick-legged sprinters that we Americans so prized. I'd heard it all before. I could quote it all verbatim.

I let it go because I loved him, without reason, loved the way he looked at me and the way he reached out a hand to brush against me when I walked past him, loved the way he let me run the place (most of the time), loved the knowledge that he gave me so freely, loved his eyes and his face and his smile and his voice, and that lovely accent wasn't bad either. How could you not love someone who put all of your dreams in your grasp, so graciously and freely? I had run away for this, I had come here for to be with racehorses, and Alexander put it all in the palm of my hand. If he was somewhat old-fashioned, it was a small price to pay.

Most of all I loved our middays, the early eleven o'clock lunch hour, where we hid from the sun and the work waiting for us outdoors. In the kitchen, we sat drinking coffee, and Alexander slumped over the high counter top of the bar between kitchen and breakfast room, poring over the print-out of the *Thoroughbred Daily News* that the secretary placed there, between the fruit bowl (early oranges from the trees in the yard) and the candy dish (today she had filled it with wrapped dark chocolate squares—which I would cheerfully eat until I couldn't sit a horse but would just wobble like a Weeble. I believed our secretary was jealous of me and wanted to ruin my figure). I loved our bright kitchen: a high-ceilinged white room, touches of gray granite. The room was lit spectacularly from the ten-foot windows in the breakfast room that looked down the hill to the training barn and the racetrack. Opulent in its simplicity, the kitchen was where we lived.

He looked restless there, unsettled, an outdoorsman in the cool gray room. He was a tow-headed Englishman yet, despite the years; decades in the sun had lightened the blond almost to white, but he insisted that there was no gray in the family, and it looked like he'd prove himself right. Tall, too tall and heavy in the shoulders to gallop the babies himself anymore, but you could see in the strong arms and hands the rider he'd once been, growing up riding to the hounds, a fearless young boy, a ruthless young man, out to win at anyone's cost, as long as it wasn't his horse's. *Nothing* would ever be as important as his horse. The same sun that had kissed his hair and eyebrows had darkened and damned his pale skin, and he was growing wrinkled—no, leathered—in that classic, long-jawed, aristocratic way of his ancestors. In the pressed khaki pants, polished brown boots, and button-down shirts that he favored, he looked the part of enterprising pinhooker or prosperous veterinarian, in the neighborhood of fifty and wheeling down towards a gin-soaked retirement on a spacious yacht somewhere in the West Indies. In reality, Alexander was simply an accomplished horseman, gambling each day on the things he knew best: Thoroughbreds, in their breeding, their raising, their breaking, and their training. He might have turned down the yacht, in fact; there were no horses at sea.

I think I would have taken it; at this moment I would have liked nothing more than to walk away from all these horses and their demands and their antics. Alexander had insisted that I go out and look at a yearling in the field, which had set the entire herd of little demons off into ecstasies of kicking and biting and carrying-on. I'd avoided the flying hooves but some little chestnut with a white face and a naughty eye had managed to bite me on the forearm, and I could tell already that the formidable bruise was going to be a work of art that would last a week. Add that to the sore spot on my rear and the necessity of driving down to Winning Edge later to buy a new hard hat to replace the one I'd hit on the concrete wall this morning, add to that Saltpeter's lameness. . . oh, just keep adding! I was exhausted with it all. I wanted to climb into my bed with a romance novel and forget all these crazy beasts. Of course, I couldn't. Alexander would remind me that after lunch, the vet was coming to check the pregnant mares. Oh, Alexander. I gazed at him guardedly, hiding my eyes beneath my lids. I still loved to watch him, no matter what his horrible beasts might have done to my life.

Of course, it wasn't entirely my fault. If you looked at me, you'd see the truth: I am the the typical American horse-crazy girl, just not quite in my teens anymore. My hair still in a blond ponytail, but the bright gold mixing with darker streaks, like a bale of orchard grass instead of clean straw. Still tall, still slim, still wearing worn jeans and untucked polo shirt with the collar half turned-up and dirty paddock boots, my uniform since I was at least twelve. It all gave me away; I was never really going to go to college, I was never going to get a job in an office, or own a pair of heels. I was a horse girl, the sort of girl that looked too light and weak to ride racehorses—but if you try to muscle a horse around, you're in for a surprise, anyway. Even my name was fancy and horsey: Alexis, shortened to Alex, which made us, yes, Alex and Alexander. Or, in Ocala parlance, Alexander and His Alex.

Yes, second, and his, always.

I suppose being twenty-five years younger and the former groom doesn't help. Maybe I was his toy, and maybe I only thought of myself as something much more, as a partner, as a friend, as a reasonably imaginative lover. I'd heard Earl Whiting say "Now, now, Betty, she makes him happy," over the cocktail shrimp at a Florida Breeders Care About Kids charity night at the Ocala Hilton, and I hadn't imagined her eyes rolling at me from down the buffet line. I was too young for the Ocala society, such as it was, and so it was just me and Alexander, which was fine until we were thrust into terribly awkward social situations like that. Which we tried to avoid. Again, there was a reason why I didn't own a pair of heels—I didn't *need* a pair of heels for this life.

It had been good for these five years, though; who was I kidding? We rattled around the big house, dirty and disheveled and content, for there was a maid every other day to tidy up our messes and sweep up our mud, and a strange entrepreneurial housewife from Gainesville who cooked things and put them in our freezer every Monday: exotic curried meatloaf concoctions, or neo-Creole lasagna, or whatever else was fashionable and featured on the Food Network, which I imagined to be her pornography. I'd eat anything she made, as long as I didn't have to touch the gleaming stainless steel appliances, especially that terrifying natural gas stovetop. Sometimes I felt overfaced by the sparkling expense of everything that surrounded me. I was a solid middle-class girl, raised in subdivisions, begging and mucking stalls for the privilege of riding other people's horses, coming home to macaroni and cheese with a side of hot dogs. This lifestyle, in this big house, on this outstanding spread of two hundred acres, was far more than I could have asked for. I mean, a horse farm! A mansion! I would have been thrilled with an aging single-wide mobile home, if there had just been room for a horse outside.

Okay, well, maybe it wasn't a mansion, but it wasn't far off. Like a lot of Florida farms, it had a history based in the very random time known as the 80s. Ocala had more Follies built in the rush of strange business and cocaine money than all the Romantic ages in England. This sprawling farmhouse looked like it had been dropped carelessly from a helicopter which had been en route to a more suitable location, like Vermont. It had been the farm manager's house when the absentee landowner was a so-called "Wealthy Industrialist," the manufacturer of random and unrelated items like breakfast cereals and tires and hair accessories. He had built this beautiful farm and yet lived, inexplicably, in Omaha, and had flown down to watch works on the professional-grade training track before sending his horses to unsuccessful careers at Belmont, at Fair Grounds, at Finger Lakes, dropping progressively in prestige, in ambition, and in cash flow. He had been living proof that you can't buy horse sense, that all the wealth in the world can't make up for a lack of breeding, human or otherwise. His horses populated rescue ranches and retired racehorse adoption programs across the country. One of them had competed at Rolex Kentucky last year, a robust fifteen-year-old, leaping unmovable logs and splashing into the infamous Duck Pond. He had come in fourth, the highest placed American team member.

Alexander slapped down the papers and sighed. "Truly Given had another stakes winner yesterday."

This was interesting news. Truly Given's first three-year-olds were just starting to win races. We had a nice chestnut colt of his in the shedrow now. His owners wanted us to send him with the next group to New York. Didn't all the owners? No one wanted to pay training rates on a horse at the training center, loafing in the shedrow, lounging under an oak tree during an afternoon's turn-out. They wanted them at the racetrack, bouncing off the walls, earning their keep. So to speak. Anyway, now they'd really be turning the heat on to

Alexander to get the horse to New York. They had too much money and clout to want to run him at nearby Tampa, where the ground was easy on the legs and the races were fun but rather second-class.

"He could go," I said cautiously. I didn't want him to, and neither did Alexander, so there was no harm in sharing that position. I watched the back of Alexander's head as he went and looked out the window, down to the training barn. If we weren't in the shedrow, we were watching it. "He was early—wasn't he a February? And it's February already. He's really and truly two now, but no one will think of racing him until summer. He'll need to get used to life at the track, get a gate card. . ."

"Rates paid to a New York trainer instead of to us," he muttered. "You want another empty stall?"

"We only have three empty stalls," I said defensively. "And we always get new trainees after the two-year-old sales. The Hastings' alone are planning on buying at least six this year,"—naming our newest, wealthiest clients, ready to play the game in a big way, already the proud owners of a new black Lexus SUV specifically for driving to the farm—"And Rick Owen always sends us his partnership's buys. He'll buy a dozen. Those are the certain ones. There will be a few stragglers. Why not make the owners happy?"

Because it went against Alexander's grain to make training decisions solely to keep owners happy, I knew. He was of a school of thought that owners were senseless louts, good only for paying the bills put before them, signing the checks their accountants wrote out, or however it was done these electronic days. I tried to ignore it.

"Horses are better off at the farm," he grumbled, and I recognized one of his pet arguments on the way. "We need a better track to ship to. I'd rather ship them in and then bring them home for turn-out than send all the good ones to Kentucky and New York to get locked up in stalls. Good horses go lame from lack of exercise. Ten minutes a morning on the training track is no way to keep a horse sound and fit, to say nothing of their brains." He shook his head and went back in for another assault on the coffee pot. "You can't explain that to these owners, a bunch of accountants who think of nothing but money and ignore the sport. When I was a boy this was the sport of kings, and now it's the sport of bankers. You can't pinch pennies and keep horses—it can't be done."

"I know, you're right," I said, trying to be soothing, before he sank into a muttering, bitter sort of mood for the rest of the workday. "We just have to do the best that we can. But Alexander, we have to have clients. We can't own them all. If it was our horse, we'd do it differently— but we don't own the horse."

"If I could change one thing about this business," he growled, "I'd get rid of all the people."

I never had much love for people, either—that was why I surrounded myself with horses—but I had enough sense to know that clients pay the bills, and if a horse was sound and going to a good trainer, at a good track like Belmont, there was no reason to worry about breaking him down. Sure, he'd miss the paddocks and a roll under the oak tree, rubbing the sand into his back, but he was going to give all that up sooner or later anyway, and it was only for a few years. The faster he ran, the shorter he'd be there. The clever horse would run like the devil was at his tail and secure himself a good stud farm position before he turned four. I tried to explain that to all my colts. But you know colts. They're *boys*. They never listen.

Alexander started a headcount of all the horses in the training barn, emptying the candy dish and lining up the foil squares in long rows on the countertop. "We'll send up six then—the Truly Given, the Smarty Jackson, those three colts of Owen's, and. . ." he paused, finger on a chocolate, trying to determine a horse's fate. "If that Holiday colt goes. . ." he faltered, trying to think of the flashy bay colt's name.

"Beachside," I supplied. It was one of my unwritten job requirements to know all the horse's names and spout them off at the correct times. Sometimes, when the barns were full to bursting before a sale, I actually had to sit and study lists of names, breeding, markings, and birthdays.

"Beachside," he agreed, nodding. He looked at the diagram he had made for himself, shook his head with displeasure, and walked back to the breakfast table, which was set prettily with white china dishes and coffee cups, as if I were going to don a gingham apron and serve biscuits and homemade sausage and scrambled eggs, instead of shoving the dishes out of the way to make room for an oversized mug of black coffee and a copy of *The Daily Racing Form.*

"And Saltpeter," he muttered, as an afterthought.

"We'll do fine with what we've got," I said, pouring more coffee. "The barn doesn't have to be full to pay for itself." One hundred and fifty dollars a day plus veterinary expenses tended to pay our training barn bills. The fee was more for Alexander's expertise than for the overhead, alarming as equine expenses always are. I topped off Alexander's cup and sat down across from him. His last sentence made its way into my brain and sat there, worrisome. "Wait—where's Saltpeter going?" That poor colt, and poor Manuel, too, icing the ankle down in the barn while we idled in the kitchen.

He just looked at me and shook his head, and I knew: he'd written the colt off for the season. My confidence that it had been just a little set-back suddenly wavered. Alexander knew more than me, after all. He'd been conditioning horses when I'd been sitting up until midnight to catch the bettor's program "Calder Report" on my parent's television, up too late on a school night, trying to sort out long-shots from favorites and the mysterious phrases like "drop in class" and "percentage off a lay-off." He'd been winning purses and end-of-year awards when I'd been learning to jump cross-rails on a school pony. Wearing me down with an excess of knowledge was never really a problem for him.

"I'll turn Saltpeter out," he said finally. "He's not mature enough. This little injury—he needs more time. That shouldn't have happened."

His face grew long, the wrinkles in it deeper than I'd seen in a while, and he looked his age. And I thought for a desperate moment that I was in love with a man too old for me.

"Don't—" I said falteringly, but there was nothing I could say. He loved Saltpeter. He had bred him for the two-year-old classics. Saltpeter was supposed to go

Saratoga this summer, make us proud. I thought fleetingly of purse money and future stud fees, mercenary, because the Thoroughbred business only pays in green linen paper, never blue or red satin rosettes. A little rest, he'd be good as new. We could catch up on lost time.

But no, it didn't matter about the money, because Alexander didn't do this work for the money. The money was a lucky happenstance of getting good horses, getting good owners, and the unlikely concurrence of doing the right thing by a horse *and* getting stakes winners. Turning out Saltpeter was certainly an overreaction to the little shortening in his stride this morning, but it was more than a trainee suffering a set-back. It was about falling in love with a horse, and that was something Alexander had rarely allowed himself to do. But Saltpeter was special. Every year, there was a horse that wriggled its way into our affections, despite all our best efforts. Last year, it had been Red Erin. Oh, Red Erin! I still couldn't let myself think of him, and I *never* mentioned him to Alexander.

This year, the beloved son was Saltpeter, due to circumstances beyond anyone's control. Saltpeter was Alexander's pet—Alexander had loved his dam, a gray mare he had imported from England, and ridden himself in the mornings. She was flawless—sweet-tempered, sound as a dollar, and fast as the wind—winning races until she was six years old. That had been fifteen years ago. She died last year, a terrible colic during her pregnancy, losing the foal that would have been Saltpeter's little brother. A chestnut with four white socks and lungs which were not ready for air. We had been up all night with her. The vet had advised euthanasia. Alexander had wiped tears from his eyes and held her wet head while the vet depressed the plunger on the syringe, while she closed her eyes and breathed her last. Great horsemen may not be sentimental, but they still love the special ones.

Saltpeter was all that was left of her. Of course Alexander wouldn't risk the gray colt, a facsimile of his perfect mother. He'd give up all the dreaming of Saratoga and wait it out until the horse was a three-year-old.

Kentucky Derby, I thought idly. We always thought of Kentucky Derby when we looked at Saltpeter. It was an affliction, this desire to win this one silly race every May. All horsemen had it, though, the Derby disease. And what prep race? He'd like the tight little turns at Gulfstream— maybe the Florida Derby. I daydreamed in workouts, in breezes, in nomination fees and purse money, of smiling for the photographer in the winner's circle. A pay-off now or a pay-off later. It was worth waiting, I supposed, though painful to sit out a season for nothing more than a twisted ankle. One dainty ankle, expected to bear a thousand pounds at forty miles an hour for a mile and more.

I shrugged it off as if it didn't affect me, as if I wasn't a partner in the farm, who was entitled to some sort of input on financial matters. And sending a horse back out to pasture when he ought to be prepping for a race was certainly a financial matter. No matter how much you tried to sugar-coat it, if your business model contains the word "horse" in it somewhere, then those horses are going to have to earn you money. They can't always gambol in shady paddocks when there is work to be done. Like people.

Anyway, my opinion would not be solicited in this, or any other matter, once he'd made his decision. Being a partner was solely on paper. It always had been, and I was feeling it more than ever. Alexander had given me a partnership two years ago, because he thought he was being kind and generous, as a reward for my hard work and slavish devotion, not because he thought that I'd make some kind of meaningful contribution to the business of breeding and training racehorses—although he did have to admit that my eye for conformation was natural and precise, and that I ran the place to perfection —perhaps not his celestial level, but pretty damn good anyway. If I didn't always feel appreciated, or respected, I didn't care—that much. I was in love with him.

I'd always been in love with him, since that first moment. Since that day I'd driven into Ocala, desperate for a job with Thoroughbreds, and seen him getting into his truck at a barbecue joint, and lost all sense or inhibition and just ran over to him to announce my undying devotion to his training skill and to beg for a job —ever since that day, I knew even as I agreed to be at the training barn at four thirty in the bloody morning, that I wasn't going to work for him just because he could teach me everything that I ever wanted to know, but because I was hopelessly in love with him, with his legend, with his face, with everything about him. Maybe it was just that I was in love with that posh English accent. At the moment, so tired of my life, so tired of these horses and this heartbreak, this exhaustion and these bruises, this monotony of sun-up to sun-down labor, it was good to blame my choices on something foolish and superficial, because it felt like a foolish and superficial decision. Falling in love with your boss, with your much older, worldlier boss, when you are a girl in your early twenties, is always a mistake. It has to be. Doesn't it?

I still loved him, though, for whatever reason. It kept me here. I looked out at the barns, felt a shudder of revulsion at the afternoon of holding up mare's tails for the vet so that he could check a dozen sets of reproductive systems, and thought that nothing else could keep me here anymore.

I leaned over and stroked the back of his neck, gently, and he reached out and pulled me to his lap. I lolled across him, arms behind his neck, hands clasped, and smiled up at him. He looked down with those crinkled eyes, as if he was looking always at the sun, and smiled back. "Lovely girl," he said softly. "Lovely little groom."

Three
Vet checks

It was hot by one o'clock, another little annoyance of Florida life—there were no guarantees in temperature in the winter. The summer was predictable as clockwork—it will be humid, it will be hot, it will storm, your power will go out—but the winter was anyone's guess. This morning it had been sixty and foggy, now it was sunny and eighty, and by tomorrow it might be thirty-five and sleeting.

I was standing in a stall door, a horse's hindquarters behind me, a bristly black tail draped over my shoulder. The mare had an annoying habit of clenching her tail down with astonishing strength, and I had an unpleasant vision of being strangled to death, pressed close against a horse's fat rear by her vindictive tailbone wrapped around my neck, rather like a boa constrictor. It probably wasn't physically possible, but you have lots of time for random daydreams when you're working your way down a row of broodmares, checking them for impending labor, or ovulation, or a confirmation of pregnancy. The tail hairs get in the way and can introduce dirt into the mare, so someone has to hold the tail securely out of the way—it just so happens that draping it over your far shoulder and holding it there tightly is the best way to do this.

The vet withdrew his arm from the mare and stripped off the manure-fouled glove that ran up to his shoulder. The sweet smell of lube mixed with the stench of grassy manure never failed to hit my gag reflex, and I had to swallow hard. It was just one of those things that I never got used to, right up there with roadkill skunk and the aroma of cooking mushrooms. At least those two I managed to avoid most of the time. There weren't an awful lot of skunks in Ocala, and Alexander wouldn't touch mushrooms with a ten-foot pole.

"Well?" I asked, untangling myself from the mare's tail. The groom inside the stall maneuvered her away from the open stall door and unbuckled her halter.

"Foal's still sitting pretty low," he said, fumbling with his ultrasound machine for the next horse, an open mare who hadn't been bred yet this season. "In the next few days, probably, you'll see a change—but I wouldn't expect him tonight."

"Wouldn't that be nice," I said dryly. "A full night's sleep on a full moon in February."

He laughed. "You hate early foals, don't you?"

"I hate being *cold*," I corrected. "And February nights are usually freezing. I like a nice warm April night for foals. But then I have a colt who is two months younger than the February babies, so what can you do?"

"That's the business," he said, shrugging along with me. "We breed them at the exact wrong time, when the grass is bad, when the nights are cold, and cost ourselves twice as much as we should in hay and worry about keeping the foal warm enough when it freezes, just so they'll be born as close to January first as possible. What can you do? If they'd change the birthday system, maybe we could have foals when nature intended, in May and June when there is grass and warm nights."

Like everyone else in Ocala, even the vet was in on the racing game, with three broodmares of his own, grazing in his big backyard, and he lived by the same arbitrary rules that we did. Thoroughbreds celebrated a mutual birthday on January first, and if your horse happened to be born later than another horse that spring, well, then you'd just have to accept the fact that your horse was younger and possibly less mature than the other one. They'd still have to race in the same age division. Horses change a lot in their first three years, and a matter of weeks could make a huge difference in their maturity and athleticism, so it was a very real problem: the question of how early you could get a mare bred, when their reproductive systems still argued that it was the dead of winter, too early to bear a foal.

"They'll never change the birthday system. Thoroughbreds will always age up on January first, because that's the way it's always been done, and those old Kentucky boys never change anything." I was sick to death of horsemen who did things a certain way because that's the way they'd always been done, and sometimes that seemed like it applied to every horseman in the world.

We went to the next stall and the groom slid open the heavy wooden door, where a petite little maiden mare was looking at us apprehensively. He went inside and haltered her, walking her around and backing her into the open doorway so that only her hindquarters peeped out. It was the traditional stance for breeding work—the doorway kept the horse from sidling back and forth while uncomfortable work was done on her nether regions. It meant that I saw so much more of the broodmares' hind ends then I ever did of their faces. I could identify them by the curvature of their rumps and the length of their tails.

"If you had a colt with just a little shortness behind, probably from turning an ankle, would your initial thought be turn-out?" I asked suddenly, gripping the bristling tail hairs expertly.

"Well," the vet thought for a moment, squirting his glove from an industrial-sized tube of generic lube, "I suppose I'd have to look at it, do some X-rays of the fetlock, ultrasound the tendons. Did… did something happen?"

"Yeah," I admitted. "Just this morning. And I was just thinking that it's weird that he would decide to turn him out without taking pictures of the joint first."

"That is weird," he mused, putting his arm into the mare's backside with an unpleasant sucking noise. The mare wiggled, alarmed by the intrusion, and the groom hissed to her *"Hush, hush,"* from inside the stall.

"I don't know what to think," I admitted. "I'm not even sure I should have mentioned it."

"Probably not, knowing Alexander," he said, feeling around inside the mare. He was up to his shoulder and we were eye-to-eye, nearly nose-to-nose. "If he's turning out the colt without asking me to look, there's another reason. Is it yours?"

"Yeah, it's ours."

"Is it that gray from his old mare?"

"Yup." This was Doctor Eddie, after all—he'd been the one who had put the needle in her vein and pressed the juice in.

"Okay then," he said. He straightened and pulled his arm out with a long slurping sound. "I think that she's got something going in there. . . I'll ultrasound and tell you if it's ready for breeding yet." He grabbed the little wand of the ultrasound, added more lube, and went in for a second exploration. "As for this colt—listen, Alexander isn't going to make rational decisions about this colt. He loved that mare. You're going to have to let him do his own thing here."

As if there was any option but Alexander's decisions. "It's not like what I say has any bearing—"

"You think that?" Eddie was surprised. "He listens to you. Believe me, he relies on you. Just—trust him on the colt. He's not a sentimental guy, you know that, but don't get in his way on this one. He's thinking with his heart and not his head. As long as he doesn't run the whole place that way, you're fine."

The heart and not the head. You couldn't run a business that way, Dr. Eddie was telling me, and I needed no reminder. We all knew that. He saw it every day in his rounds, people making sentimental decisions and spending small fortunes on horses who would never recover, and people making sensible decisions and putting down the horses who would forever be out of work. Businesses are run with the head and not the heart. That's just harder with horses, but that's the way it has to be.

Four
Cast

The phone buzzed in my hip pocket at nine o'clock that night, when we were both yawning in front of the television in the living room, and I pulled it out with uncharacteristic urgency. Not many people called my personal line—it was possibly a family emergency, more likely a stable emergency.

"TRAINING BARN" blinked on the display. *"Shit!"* I told the phone. Alexander looked over and lifted his eyebrows, waiting for me to answer it.

"Alex?" It was Raul, the night watchman.

"What's going on?"

"It's the gray colt—Saltpeter. He get cast and he bang up his leg real bad. No weight on it."

"Oh my *god.*" I slapped the display, the twenty-first century equivalent of slamming the phone in the receiver, and leapt up from the sofa. "Come on, Saltpeter got cast and he's not putting weight on one of his legs. No, I *don't* know which one!" I ran for the front door, pausing to slip on my boots bare-footed, feeling with disgust all the hay and straw and gravel that had worked into them throughout the day, grinding into the soles of my feet. I held the door open for Alexander and we ran for the golf cart together.

The barn was lit up and all the horses were in a state, awakened from their sleep and upset by the break in their routine. There was whinnying and neighing between the stalls, between the barn and the paddocks, between the paddocks and the further pastures. The whole farm was a din of shouting horses, wanting to know why on earth their peace had been shattered. Pretty soon it would spread, farm to farm, across the whole countryside. One cast horse could mean square miles of alarmed herds, whole ZIP codes of equines on alert.

Raul was waiting for us in front of Saltpeter's stall, his friendly face drawn. He was the nicest of our grooms, the best-spoken, the best-educated, the best horseman of them all, and he chose to work nights, when ninety-nine nights out of one hundred he spoke to no one, shared his knowledge with no one, displayed his impressive skill with horses to the stars and the moon alone. We dreaded seeing him, because we only heard from him on the hundredth night, when disaster struck, in the form of colics or fevers or the ridiculous, *stupid* disaster that could result from a cast horse.

"I hear banging and run down, see him up against the wall," he explained rapidly, standing aside so we could get into the stall. "And he been banging his left hind up against the wall. I grab his forelegs to pull him away, but he been there kicking and—you see—"

We did see. Three-legged-lame, the gray colt stood with the toe of his left hind hoof just delicately scraping the surface of the straw bedding, which had been thrown wildly around the stall by his thrashing attempts to get away from the wall. Twelve by twelve feet, the standard size of a horse stall, still isn't that much room for a thousand-pound, six-foot-tall animal; anyway, a horse can lay down to roll in exactly the wrong place and find himself trapped against a wall even in the largest space. Getting "cast" was usually heralded by a succession of bangs as a panicking horse slammed his body against the wall, trying to get enough space to get his legs beneath him so that he could rise, and most of the time we would come running into the stall just in time to see the wild-eyed horse gain purchase against the wall and shove himself away so that he could get himself up. But if they couldn't help themselves, someone had to go in and grab whatever leg was handy, to drag the horse's bulk a few feet from the wall. When you had to go to this extreme, the horse was usually in enough of a state that he'd already hurt himself—as Saltpeter clearly had.

And it was the *left* hind. The one he'd gone off on early this morning, after the runaway incident. I watched it, frozen with horror. I felt like I could see the fetlock swelling before my eyes. As for Alexander—I hazarded a glance to my left, where he still stood in the doorway—he looked frozen, his face blank, as if he wasn't able to take in this deepening disaster surrounding his favorite horse. Everyone has their limits, I thought. Red Erin last year, Saltpeter's dam the year before—all his favorite children were being struck down. There was a sudden silence in the barn; the horses stopped neighing, Raul's Labrador stopped barking, the whip-poor-wills in the woods behind the barn were silent. We waited for Alexander. The whole world was waiting on Alexander.

"Will he walk on it at all?" Alexander snapped out, breaking the spell. A yearling in a far paddock shouted for his mates and started the cacophony up again. "Step him forward for me."

Raul took the horse's halter and gave a gentle tug. The colt leaned forward as long as he could, resisting the pull, before taking a hopping step forward, keeping the hind leg as immobile as he could. It wasn't just the leg—it was the joint, that bulging little ankle. It wasn't just that he wanted to keep weight off of his leg, he didn't want to *flex* his leg.

Alexander shook his head. "No more, stop," he told Raul. He went forward and ran his hand down the leg, wincing as Saltpeter flinched but stopped short of kicking at him; kicking would have required too much movement. "He's not a delicate horse," he said from down in the straw. "He's not the kind of horse to think he's dying when he's got a little scrape."

"He's got heart," I agreed. It was one of our favorite things about him, his big heart, a will to keep moving, a desire to win. Racehorses needed it, show jumpers needed it, polo ponies needed it—it was the most essential quality in a good horse, and the most indefinable —*heart*.

Alexander stood up and rested a hand on the colt's hip. "Ice boot, please, Raul," he said. "I'll have the vet out directly, but in the meantime, put some hay in front of him and get that ice boot on as gently as you can."

Raul nodded and ducked out of the stall. I watched him go with regret. He was an incredible horseman, but he only used his gifts when things went wrong.

Five
Another ending

I cried.

Alexander cried.

We buried him in the cow pasture. Red Erin had died after a tropical depression had soaked the ground for days; we couldn't dig a hole to bury him in without dipping into the bursting water table, and we'd had to cremate him. But now it was the dead of winter, the dry season, the ground rock-hard and cold, and Manny took the backhoe out and dug the hole. Like last year, and the year before, we watched as the handyman and the grooms removed the front wall of the stall, wrapped the corpse in a tarp, and dragged away our favorite to be slid into the grave that was waiting for him.

"It's a freak thing," Dr. Eddie had said, looking at the X-rays. "It's just one of those terrible things. But the bone here is absolutely in pieces. There's nothing to screw together. It *might* fuse. . ."

"If he can get through the cast and the stall rest, you mean," Alexander said, finishing his sentence for him.

"Yes," Eddie said, laying down the photo. "It doesn't look good."

"Red Erin didn't get through it," Alexander said softly, shaking his head. He leaned across the desk of the spotless tack room, rubbing his hands on the mahogany top, following the swirls of the grain. I sat clutching the arms of the wooden chair in the corner, my feet against the desk leg, my head in the corner of the walls, looking for a nest where I could hide. Alexander was distant from me, more my boss than my lover, and I felt cold and tired and lonely. It was three o'clock in the morning and all I could think of was Red Erin, and the day he had died, gray and wet with the hot humid wind off the Gulf of Mexico blowing into the stall, and the dirty, weeks-old cast that still encased his foreleg, from the crazy, freak injury to his foreleg. That leg didn't kill him—the other three did, the hooves slowly dissolving inside as inflammation broke down the tissue, rotated the interior bones, and pierced the sole of the foot. He had died in agonies, with our tears mingling with his sweat, and I knew that would never be allowed to happen again. Saltpeter would die quietly, before the sun rose again.

Eddie went out to his truck to put away his X-ray machine and get out the syringe and the bottle.

"There's no time or reason for a second opinion," Alexander said to me. "Look at that bone. It's in little pieces. He'll never stand on that leg again."

I gazed down at the ghostly image of the colt's inner workings, all the detailed little machinery of joints that slid together so flawlessly to create the perfect athlete. Something so strong and so fluid! Horses could never be reproduced by a man's hand; no artist could ever do them justice, no machinist could ever engineer something that married beauty and efficiency so perfectly, but that beauty was marred by its own delicacy and perfection: one tiny jolt to its lacey structures and everything collapsed like dominoes, like a demolished building, one long terrible implosion, and all that was left was a ruined animal waiting to be put out of its misery.

"This is unbearable," I said to the dying leg on the transparent sheet.

"It is unbearable," Alexander said. "But horses die."

He put his head down on the desk, temple to the wood, and we sat in silence, separate. I should have turned to him to comfort him. I should have put my hand on his shoulder, I should have kissed his neck, I should have told him I loved him. But I looked away from him, across the room, to where a mirror hung in a gilt frame, elegantly surrounded by trophies and win photos from the horses we had sent to the races, as if it were the drawing room of a landed aristocrat. I watched my reflection, my three a.m. reflection, my 23-hours-of-wakefulness-face so wary and tired and sad. I was tired of being tired. I was tired of being sad. I was tired of horses and all their heartbreaks. I turned away from Alexander, then, and I got up and left the room, and sat in the golf cart, swatting at mosquitoes in the chill, until he came and sat down next to me, and we wordlessly drove back to the house.

Six
Closed curtains

If Alexander noticed that I had stopped talking, he didn't bring it up. He was too busy maintaining a silent funk of his own. We did the things we had always done, but we ignored one another. We stepped around one another in the kitchen, in the living room, in the bedroom, in the barns. We were polite, and we were icy. It was grief, and disappointment, and exhaustion, I told myself. We had both had a long winter, and the sooner we could get through the selected two-year-old sale, unloading a dozen or so horses from our personal breeding program that we didn't plan on running ourselves, and accepted the new boarders (which were sometimes the same horses that we shipped to Miami to be sold), the better off we would be. Alexander wasn't above slipping away mid-breeding season for a weekend in the Keys; we had to keep our phones on our persons at all times, in case there was a calamity with a mare or foal or one of the trainees, but it was better than the alternative that most horsepeople were faced with: spending the breeding season, January to June, locked down on the farm.

"Horsemen have miserable love lives," he'd told me once. "Sometimes you have to get away right at the peak of things, to remind you of who is most important in your life."

I waited for some mention of a bed and breakfast booked, of picking out some new music or a book to listen to on the long journey south, but nothing happened, and we went wheeling through February, with the breeding sheds open, three dozen horses in training, and the death lingering between us. The sales horses shipped out, the empty stalls were raked back and left to air, snowed white with lime. Two foals were born on the coldest night of the year, the pastures sparkling with frost, and I shivered under three sweaters while I tied up the placentas with hay-twine and a plastic bag of sand, to help speed its expulsion from the mares, while they licked their wet foals and grumbled contentedly. Another was born on a sunny afternoon in a gray patch of sand in the middle of the paddock; the other mares held their distance while the veteran mama laid down, pushed out her foal in a matter of minutes, and hopped up to graze while the baby scrabbled in the sand. I pulled the foal into the cleaner grass so that its nostrils wouldn't get clogged with wet dirt and went about the usual business, dousing the navel stump with iodine, tying up the placenta, and then sat in the grass to soak up a little warmth from the sun while the foal got to work at controlling his four stilt legs.

Alexander watched from the kitchen window.

I could see him. I looked away, back at the foal. I was not interested in its efforts to stand, or find its mother's udder. I knew it had to, because that was my job, to make sure the foal had a good start, survived, grew up strong. But I didn't have any real feelings for it anymore. And clearly Alexander did not either, or he'd have come out to check on its progress.

The curtains twitched closed. I saw them without trying, I saw them because I had to look. We never closed those curtains. I closed my eyes for a minute, to blot out the sun and the grass and the foal and the house where Alexander had hidden himself.

Everything was going wrong.

Seven
Erin's Princess

Some rituals did not change. Only the new silence defined them. In the mid-afternoon, we came inside to drink another pot of coffee and watch a few races, fending off the afternoon's drowsiness. It was the most challenging part of the day, worse than getting out of bed at four thirty in the morning to get to the training barn, worse than heading back out to the broodmare barns and the yearling barns to check the conditions after we had changed out of training clothes and the day was heating up, worse than business calls in the office at five thirty in the evening, a time calculated to provide the maximum number of voicemail calls and a minimum of actual time-consuming person-to-person communications (businessmen were out of the office for the night; horsemen were at the races or presiding over night feeding). The afternoon doldrums and the prospect of still more work before nightfall were enough to put anyone off the equestrian lifestyle.

I had started to just give in and slip off to sleep, sideways on the couch, while the race calls echoed in my dreams. There had been a foal the night before, another long birth from a maiden mare who didn't understand what was happening to her. She thought she was going to die, probably, and when the first contractions struck her in mid-afternoon she flung herself around the huge foaling stall like a maniac fighting off a strait-jacket. In the end the foal had been large and poorly presented, and it had taken Dr. Eddie at two a.m. to reach in, grab the leg that was caught behind her pelvis, and pull the big colt free. He was coming back this evening to stitch her up; the colt's big shoulders had torn her on the way out. It was enough to make you swear off children forever, all this blood and groaning and raw flesh. I thought about going up to the bedroom and slipping between the sheets, getting away from the bronze horses dancing atop the bookshelves and the race callers droning on and on with necks and lengths and under the whip and bids for the lead, away from *horses* for just a little while. . .

"Whoa!" Alexander shouted, startling me out of the coma I'd been slipping into. "Who is that?"

In-between races, when they could find absolutely nothing else to fill the airwaves with, the racing channel very occasionally showed interviews and little vignettes of racetrack life with various trainers. Dancing down a training track, black and lithe as a panther, a young colt filled the screen and then galloped out of the camera angle, which panned back to the trainer, a leathery man that I recognized as a mid-level claimer type from the New York tracks. He was very talented at picking up cheap horses on the climb, fixing them up, patching their problems (they all had problems) and turning them into expensive claimers that were, in turn, claimed by higher-echelon trainers who ran the horses in stakes races and got a great deal of money and credit for it all. The man had a curse for a talent. But at least he was earning a decent living, and he got respect from his fellow trainers, if not from the moneyed elite who purchased the high-end horses.

". . .Picked up a few two-year-olds privately from a closing breeding farm and they're turning out good..." he was saying, rather expansive and tell-all for a racehorse trainer. The interviewer asked him about the colt now pulled up behind him, flashing polished hooves in the dark gray of Aqueduct's frost-proof inner track, steaming from his fluttering nostrils. "Oh, he's a Tiger Tiger. . . Not the most fashionable sire, but out of a good Northern Dancer mare—you remember Erin's Princess, don't you, very big in the stallion stakes a few years ago."

The interviewer, a New Yorker with a long memory, began to expound in detail upon Erin's Princess, who evidently had several thrilling wins in the New York-breds restricted division as a three and four-year-old, more than a decade ago, and the colt disappeared back towards the barns. Without warning, the view cut suddenly to the post parade at Gulfstream Park, a Florida track which sparkled amidst high-rise condos in Hallandale Beach, and the cold, wind-whipped horses and trainers of Queens were replaced with palm trees, Spanish architecture, and tinkling fountains. The horses here were sweating even beneath close-clipped coats, and the railbirds wore baseball caps and sandals. Despite the pageantry, it was an unimpressive race; the horses were cheap and one favorite easily out-classed them all.

I thought about the name of the broodmare. Erin's Princess. . . there was something. . . *oh.*

"Alexander!" I exclaimed urgently. "Erin's *Princess*, for god's sake!"

Alexander turned to look at me, and his eyes were bright with sudden excitement. "You're right! That's him!"

We'd looked in vain for the last Erin's Princess colt last year, when Red Erin died of laminitis. Her two-year-old chestnut colt had been our darling, and and when he'd fractured a bone in his foreleg we'd gone to great lengths to surgically repair it, only to have him die during his confinement after surgery. It had been horrific, to come down to the barn one morning, waiting for him to poke his head over the webbing, and instead hear a terrible groaning, like a man who'd been beaten and left for dead, and rush down to find him lying in the straw with wide eyes and vein-popping sweat, in agonies from his inflamed hooves.

I'd watched when the vet slipped the needle in, two days later. I'd watched him take his last breaths, and run my hand beneath his mane, along his hot, wet neck. I'd brushed my hands over his eyelids, taken a piece of straw out of his forelock, laid the tarp over him before the front of the stall was winched off and the tractor chains were brought out to haul him out to the cow pasture. The common wisdom is that you never euthanize a horse in his stall, but Alexander would rather dismantle the barn than put his horse through more pain.

After Red Erin had died, I thought the only thing that would please me was his little brother, whom we had seen by her side at the farm in Williston, a town a few miles east. But he'd been sold privately, without the paper trail of a public auction, and we hadn't been able to locate him.

That was his glorious self on our TV screen, for just a few seconds.

"I may need you to go to New York," he announced.

I was wide awake for the first time in days, maybe weeks. "When?"

"Tomorrow? I'm not sure. But you go ahead and pack an overnight bag and ask Sandy to look up a good flight for you to JFK. Let me get a hold of this fellow and get an appointment. Dick Figaro. What a name. I'm sure Nickie knows him—"

And just like that, Alexander was off, all the misery of the past weeks completely shaken away. Into the office, to call Nickie over at Sun Meadows Training Center, the horseman who knew all horsemen, big and small.

I went upstairs and pulled out a leather carry-on, with the farm's logo embossed on the side, and started sorting through the closet, looking for sweaters and hats and gloves. It was cold in New York. I'd have to find some things that looked decent; doubtless Alexander would set me up with dinner with some of his friends, and we'd be somewhere in Manhattan, where they could show off to the country bumpkin from Down South. I didn't want to look the part of homeless jockey, even if that was the role I tended to affect in Ocala. (That's an exaggeration, and I admit it. After all, I try to look decent. I always put on clean jeans when I go somewhere in town. Besides the feed store.)

Riffling through my closet, I tried to feel some sort of excitement, that we had found the colt at last, but it just wasn't there. I didn't *want* to go to New York. I mean, I wanted to go, but I didn't. I wanted the Erin's Princess colt. Not quite as desperately as I had last year, of course. We were over the initial grief, which had been a raw and strange thing. Horses die. We knew that. We lost a yearling or a foal every year; once in a while, we lost a broodmare or a young horse in training. Horses did stupid things, horses went out of their way to hurt themselves, horses were delicate in their birth and in their pregnancies. It was part of the business. We'd loved Red

Erin—there had just been something about it him, something from the moment we saw him as a naughty red yearling—and he'd been our special pet. Of course we would have wanted to buy his brother, keep a little piece of him close to us.

It might have been different if I thought Red Erin's brother would have had the power to fix us—give me back my passion, give Alexander back his spark—and we could have gone on as we had before. But that didn't seem likely. I kicked a pair of boots aside in my closet to reveal—more boots. That was all I had. Boots, breeches, jeans. I had *nothing.* Red Erin and Saltpeter, they were nothing but reminders that horses *die,* and they are rude and dirty and stop you from doing anything else in life but worrying over them, and I was tired of them, bone-tired soul-tired *tired* of them.

I didn't want to go to New York, because I didn't want to come home again.

I hadn't been to New York alone since the summer before I came to Ocala. It was like another version of me, someone I'd almost forgotten, someone I felt nostalgic for now. I'd gone and walked the streets, refusing to use a guidebook in case someone mistook me for a tourist, when *clearly* I was a woman walking the streets of her soul's birth. I strolled Central Park in the moonlight and basked in the glow of Midtown, I rode the subway where it came bursting out of the ground somewhere high in upper Manhattan to go rattling across bridges and above the streets, I ventured across the Brooklyn Bridge and felt wonderfully dangerous to be walking the mean streets of Brooklyn alone—until I came to a Banana Republic and a Children's Place across the street from one another.

I thought, I'm going to live here. This is where writers live, and I will be a writer, and this is where I will live, and I will meet people and make friends and we will sit around and write together, in coffee shops, and then when we are done writing we will go to bars and drink and listen to music and everything will be glamorous all the time. I was going to be a writer in New York City. That was the plan. Of course, it had been a silly plan. There would be no horses in my life there. It was a fun dream while it lasted, but I quickly wrote it off once I was back in Florida, surrounded by fields of horses. Naturally I couldn't live without horses!

Now, sitting on the edge of my bed, surveying the sad truth of my wardrobe of jeans and breeches and argyle boot socks, I wondered if it had all been so much drama. Oh, I can't *live* without horses! Such an exclamation! Was that really true? Could anyone simply *not live* without horses? That seemed terribly dramatic and grade school. Maybe I just didn't want to grow up, out-grow my pony stickers and my fairy tales.

This life I led was my dream. It was supposed to be perfect. I was living the life I'd dreamed of since elementary school. Should priorities change, somewhere between elementary school and adulthood?

In the past few years, Alexander had taken me to New York several times, on jaunts to visit trainer friends. We'd gone to Belmont Park and sat in the echoing stands, built for fifty thousand and occupied by fifty on a sunny June day, the white clouds scudding above the great expanse of turf and dirt of the mile and half oval, with jets swooping low on approach to JFK. Beyond the backstretch, the silver cars of the Long Island Rail Road rattled by. It was a graceful oasis in the drama of New York City, just outside the border of Queens, and it was largely ignored, like most of North America's racetracks, by the surrounding populace.

We'd gone to Central Park (in the daylight, how conventional) and I'd admired the bomb-proof ponies of Claremont Riding Academy, jogging along the Bridle Path and weaving in and out of human joggers and dog walkers, who were in turn offended by the presence of the horses as if they weren't sure what the word "Bridle" actually meant. Perhaps they thought it meant a wedding path. Perhaps they'd thought it was a typo.

We'd shoved and tussled our way through Times Square and I had been amazed by the bored police mounts, dozing with one leg cocked and ears at half-mast, in the center of the most frenzied pedestrian and automobile jam-ups one could imagine outside of Southeast Asia.

Perhaps, I thought, digging through the dresser drawers for the thickest socks I could find, I didn't really know New York. My knowledge was based on that one solo trip and a few cursory tourist explorations with Alexander. And the horses who lived there. But wasn't that just typical? Wasn't that just like me? What else was there, but horses? What else was there to me? Horses, and horses, and more horses. Run away from home, run away from school, run to the horses. And here I was, on a farm in Ocala, where for all I knew I might live out my days (although Alexander would have to leave me the farm for that to happen, for if I wasn't killed galloping some fool yearling, I'd certainly out-live him). I was twenty-five.

I sat down hard on the bed and thought about that.

Twenty-five, no college degree, on the farm where I'd live forever, living the life I'd live forever. Up at four thirty, forever. Galloping babies in the morning, forever (or at least as long as I was limber). Holding mares for the vet in the afternoon, calling clients, leaving voicemails, dreading call-backs. Forever. Just the smell of veterinary lube and manure mixed together on a long plastic glove was enough to put me off the thought of another day of breeding season, let alone a lifetime of springs like this one.

I pushed my hair back from my face, groping for the rubber band I kept on my wrist, to pull it all away into a pony tail. The band caught on the dry ridges of my fingers. I rubbed at them, disgusted by the dirt that had ground into them. My fingers were practically black with dirt. I hadn't noticed before.

My eyes rose and trailed over the sad, dull array of clothes hanging in my closet, nothing suitable for a night out in New York, and I thought suddenly of music and nice clothes and the respect of those around me, not just horse people but real, live, living people, to whom life was more than getting up at four thirty and galloping a bunch of putzy, head-tossing, snot-nosed horses and then helping a veterinarian stick his arm up a broodmare's arse to make sure she was pregnant and making more putzy, head-tossing, snot-nosed horses, whom I would have to stay up all night waiting for and probably roll around in the straw trying to tug out of the mare, covered with amniotic fluid and blood and manure—and I wondered what the hell I was doing.

I laid back on the bed and felt very sorry for myself.

Alexander came in.

"What are you playing at?" he asked, standing in the doorway.

I rolled around and looked at him. "Do I have to go to New York?"

He nodded. "You do. I can't come with you. Too much going on here for us both gone, new horses coming in from the sales, but—" he softened, and the lines crinkled around his eyes, and my heart melted a little— "I'll miss you, you know. I wouldn't send you if it wasn't important. And your eye—you have such an eye, my dear. You'll know if he's the real thing or not. We don't *have* to have him—but I think he'll be worthwhile, and you'll know. And I really will miss you."

I smiled despite myself. It was just as nice to know he thought I had a good eye as it was to hear that he'd miss me. "Will you? But who will ride for me? We have too many horses for five riders."

"Oh," he looked about the room, thinking. "Julio can ride," he said. "He's been asking. Doesn't like the horses at Middleton, says they're half-wild. I'll call him later. Anyway, Amy is setting up a flight for you first thing in the morning, and you can go to dinner tomorrow night with Jim Tilden, you know, the trainer with that nice Twisty Humor filly that won last week, you met him at Gulfstream last year—"

"Isn't he about seventy-five, always wears that tweed cap like he's a groom at Newmarket in 1892?" I interrupted. I was not a fan of Alexander's old trainer buddy. He'd come across as a self-obsessed, lecherous old creepy—really exactly what you'd expect of a racehorse trainer of his generation—but he'd taught Alexander a lot as a young man, so I put up with him as a courtesy.

"That's right," Alexander said defensively, suspecting my thoughts and not impressed. "He's very good, he can teach you a lot. I keep trying to get him to come down for a month or two; I'd love to pair the two of you up. . . and he's good company as well."

"Fine," I said, not ready to fight about it, even though just once, just once I would have liked to have dinner with someone closer to my own age, and perhaps they could be a teensy bit less good for me, perhaps not come to the table with a five-part discourse rehearsed and ready on the subject of the influence of the inner dirt track at Aqueduct, or the best sprinters of 1975 and the very unique bridling techniques that had made them champions. "Where will we go? What should I wear?"

"Oh I don't know. Take your best, certainly, he's had a very good year and he'll take you somewhere nice."

"I don't have any best, Alexander, I've got breeches and jeans and polo shirts."

He looked at my closet, then at the suitcase sprawled nearly empty on the floor. It was packed with socks and underwear and nothing else. "Well, then buy something when you get in. You don't have to go out to the track until the next day. Enjoy Thursday in the city, and then Figaro will show you the colt on Friday morning.

He threw a black polo shirt from the pile of clean clothes on the easy chair in the corner. "I like you in that."

"That's a plain black shirt," I said doubtfully. It was, in fact, identical to the one I was wearing now, minus the gray horsehairs and bits of alfalfa and the aroma of horse sweat.

"You look fantastic in a plain black shirt," he said, smiling. "That's how I like you best. Plain and simple. You're a real horsewoman, Alex, do you know that? And you don't need any trappings. You're at your best in jeans and a plain black polo. Don't go wishing you were someone else when you're up there, darling. You're exactly who you are."

It was dramatic and grade school of me, I know, but as he went out of the room, I thought, *neither of us have any idea who I am.*

Eight
First impressions of New York

Oh, how predictably, the flight was a nightmare.

Flying from Orlando is a special kind of purgatory for the person who hates both airplanes and being in close proximity to small, sugared-up, overstimulated children. Even on the eight a.m. flight to JFK, the airplane was packed. Exhausted, red-eyed, sunburned, the parents who had spent thousands for a week at the theme parks fought for overhead compartment space to wedge their diaper bags and bursting shopping bags from outlet malls and Disney souvenir shops. The children scrambled about underfoot, looking for window seats at all costs, wailing for toys that had been stashed away already, causing their parents to climb up again once we'd all seemed to have found our seats, to dig through the packed bags for that one action figure or stuffed doll that could make or break their child's day.

I wearily gave up my back seat, where the roar of the engines would have combined with my headphones to drown out the shrieking, to a twelve-year-old who had been assigned a wing seat. Here the window labeling gravely informed me of my responsibilities: like some sort of scout leader, it was my role in the unlikely event that we survived a crash to open the window, produce a slide, and mother hen the other passengers out of the burning wreckage. I glanced at the instructions and then slid on my headphones, regretting the amount of coffee I'd already had that morning. No chance of a nap, then, as I had thoughtlessly filled my veins with caffeine.

Thankfully, it was only two hours to New York, and we were blessed with tailwinds that made the airplane go ridiculously fast. I'm not sure why the little in-seat monitors were equipped with speedometers. There are some things I do not need to know, and one of them is that I am traveling at six hundred miles per hour. I sighed and switched the television station to the Today Show, live from New York. The weather forecast was—wait for it—snow. I couldn't believe it.

It only snows during depressing trips to New York City in the movies and in novels, never in real life—or so I had thought. I had the uncomfortable impression that I was sinking into some sort of dramatic film that would end up airing overnights on forgotten cable networks, interspersed with ads for upside-down tomato-plant-pots and miraculously sharp chef's knives. You know, with the kind of plot where everything goes wrong and the heroine dies in the end, something nice like that.

We sank through the gray clouds and onto the still-grayer earth, without even a soul-stirring glimpse of the city skyline to raise my spirits. The snow fell in little riddles and currents of air, dancing outside of the airplane window, melting on the thick glass, while very cold-looking ground crew waved the airplane on its painfully slow route to an open gate.

JFK was unlovely and unfriendly. It was hard to imagine that I might have liked it, anyway, even if instead of a vast spread of dirty tile and strangely European-looking directional signs, scattered with humanity in various states of sorrowful leave-taking and excited holiday-making, it had been some beautiful fairyland of potted palms and hanging vines and rushing waterfalls (sort of like the Orlando airport, actually). I had been in this airport half a dozen times, and every time but the first time, I'd been in the company of Alexander—could I help it if I felt a stab of loneliness for his presence at my side, even though I felt like I needed a life-long vacation from him and his damn horses more than I needed air in my lungs? I would have appreciated it if my heart and my mind would stop sending me such utterly opposing messages; and the fact that my stomach, the primary player in any feeling of lonesomeness or homesickness, was joining in on the fun did not excite me.

The best thing that I could do was get out quickly. I had managed to smuggle my bag into the cabin and stashed it into the bursting-full overhead compartment, and so I was mercifully spared the wait for the bag to come around the crowded carousels. And I was armed with an American Express card, so instead of hauling the bag up the escalators and into the strange, wailing electric train car that ran in a circuit around the whole huge airport, I was able to go straight out of the terminal, gasping as I was exposed to the teeth of the wind, and run across about ten feet of pavement, and slide into the backseat of a black town car, waiting as if it had been put there for my express purpose. I don't know if someone else had ordered it, or if it was waiting for fares, and I did not then and I do not now care. It was *cold.*

The driver spoke just enough English to ask where to, and I gave him the hotel name, somewhere odd and offbeat south of Grand Central, in one of the hilly mansion-lined streets where Alexander's tweedy moneyed friends strolled with their jacketed terriers to private parks gated by wrought iron and carven locks.

The town car was quiet against the apparent noise of the teeming streets without, and I tried to sleep and ignore what to my eyes could only be described as squalor, but of course I leaned against the window in the end, fascinated: house after identical house with those strange gambrel roofs, just enough space between them for a sidewalk, some with swing sets wedged into tiny backyards, or barking dogs on chains, until the yards disappeared, and the sidewalks grew tinier, and the space between as well, and there was brick, brick, brick upon brick apartment house, and then shattered warehouses which looked held together with nothing more than their graffiti murals, and then the girding of a tremendous bridge and the East River and Manhattan, glittering and siren and gleaming with promise, even against the leaden gray sky and its little bursts of flurries which came swirling around at odd intervals.

We descended from the bridge and the heights above the buildings to the chaos of street-level. It was like being in a dark, narrow valley down there, below the Art Deco sculptings of the skyscrapers, in the shadows lit by neon "open" signs and rainbowed awnings of storefronts. We flashed through the streets, a dark trench-coated presence amidst the shiny yellow cabs, and turned off the avenue onto a side-street gray with winter-bare trees, pulling up at last before an imposing stone house with a spotted brass plate next to its front doors which read "Parkview Hotel."

For all its Gramercy-Park-historical-district charm, the Parkview Hotel was no retreat of the rich and famous but a Holiday Inn disguised as a boutique. The check-in clerk, seated behind a mahogany desk with ferocious clawed feet, was a bored Jersey girl with the requisite brunette ringlets and a fuchsia sweater which clashed violently with the wine-and-cream English country house decorating scheme. She was relentlessly stereotypical. She actually snapped her gum as she looked up my reservation. I almost asked her how she did it, but managed to restrain myself. I'd never heard anyone snap gum before except for people named "Doris" or "Flo" in fifties movies. It was a nice little piece of atmosphere for the Parkview's stifling attempt at timelessness.

The elevator was nice, though, not the little two-man jobs I had experienced in other historical buildings which scared the absolute life out of me—I am a dedicated, lifelong claustrophobic —but a full-size box with those fancy grill doors. I was perking up, coming out of my instinctual fear of the lure of the city and its complete and utter difference from the farm where I'd woken up this morning, when I stepped out into the corridor and located my room.

I let the door swing open. It went ninety degrees and stopped with a shuddering thud against the plastic stopper mounted on the narrow wall. There was a tiny hallway, a door into a little bathroom, a room large enough for a double bed and a dresser. If you were skinny enough, like me, to walk between the dresser and the bed, you could look out the window onto the street below. There was a pigeon on the windowsill, making its strange little purr as it promenaded back and forth. Some view. It was winter. I should be looking out at an electric-blue sea pounding on a beach studded with coconut palms. But this place? Oh, it was a decaying urban Holiday Inn closer to the Arctic Circle than the Equator. Quite a trade-off.

Well, who was I to care? I'd been brought up thinking Holiday Inn was pretty much as good as life got; it was only the past five years with Alexander that had given me champagne taste. Funny, with all the manure and dirt and hard ground and rain running down my neck that life with Alexander entailed, I supposed I got quite a lot of luxury as well. I hadn't been brought up to expect an annual week in the British Virgin Islands, or the quick weekend getaways to quiet Victorian houses in the Keys, but there you had it: I was getting shirty because I felt entitled to more than two nights in a shabby hotel room by myself during a dirty New York City snowfall.

I threw my bag with some disgust onto the bed, shaking my head at the room's size, which might have passed for a breakfast room in a double-wide trailer back in Ocala, and the chipped and battered reproduction furniture, that brought to mind more a bad period for interior design in the 1980's than the gaslight era it was meant to evoke. Oh well. What were rooms for, but for sleeping in? I had an American Express card that I didn't pay the bills for—not directly, anyway—and it was noon and I hadn't had lunch yet. I would unpack and find some warmer clothes—the leather jacket I had tossed over a short-sleeved shirt would not suffice out there with the temperature near freezing and the wind whipping through the tunneled streets—and off I would go, to find some food and acclimate myself to the city.

Nine
The city and horses

It was surprisingly easy to find my way around, despite the years since my solo trip—and despite my long-standing strict rule to walk the streets with neither a guidebook nor a map, so as not to give myself away as a tourist. I don't know why I have a horror of being found out as a tourist—it must have something to do with having grown up in Florida, where tourists are regarded with the same mutinous glares as power plants and boat factories. We know they are necessary to our survival, but they are intrusive and polluting. So I had rules for myself: don't look up too often, consult maps only in the privacy of your phone screen, and never ask directions. It's limiting in some sprawling, poorly-planned places, like, say, Tampa, but it works in New York. The grid system its roads were built upon ought to have been copied in every city in the world, defying triangles and curves—except for the venerable Broadway, and in the old labyrinthine alleyways of lower Manhattan and Greenwich Village, where crooked roads echoed paths where farmers had driven carts and cattle had watered at long-lost streams.

I thought I'd like to find my way towards the Village, where Alexander had once taken me to hear jazz in a club in a converted garage, or maybe to the leafy streets of the Upper West Side, where his cousin had a townhouse. Here, people sat out on their porches with a beer or a glass of wine and called out to their neighbors as they walked by with their dogs. The blocks felt like little villages. I thought about it as I walked cross-town, the long blocks that run east-west, until I was at Broadway and had to make a decision. I decided on uptown, and snagged a bagel and a coffee before I found a subway to take me to Lincoln Center, and then I climbed up to walk Broadway to West 72nd Street, peeping down each side street with quiet longing. If I ever had the courage to leave Ocala, I thought, this was where I'd want to live.

And what if I did it? I let myself think about the possibility. I could walk away. It *would* take courage, I reflected with mounting excitement. It would take courage to leave behind everything I knew, everything I'd built my life around, and do something new. But wouldn't it be worthwhile? What was I doing with my life? Shoving around horses before they shoved me? Training horses to run very quickly so that they could earn money? That seemed almost criminal, suddenly. There weren't very many flattering ways to look at it. I could have done anything with my life—I was smart, I was clever, I was gifted—so why wasn't I doing something *important?* Why wasn't I doing something that would leave a lasting impact in the world, something more than a name carved into a gold-plated trophy, or even a notation in the record books. That would be nice, alright, but what difference would it make, in the end? Was that really what I was going to use my brains for, to make horses run faster, to make horses earn money? It was *absurd,* that's what it was. And it was sad. I could do better than this.

And here—here was the place to run to. New York City! The home of ideas, the home of innovation! I could get a studio apartment, I could crawl up into a loft bed, I could eat take-out Chinese food at two a.m., I could write a great book which would shake the literary world on its foundations, I could.

And when I wasn't doing those three very specific things? There would be time to fill. I had a handy skeptic's voice and it wasn't afraid to make itself known now, in my time of crisis. *And what would you have here?* it wondered, walking in the shadow of huge apartment houses, their granite facades tooled with gargoyles and animals, feet pointed towards the Museum of Natural History. *Who would you know, what would you do?* it pondered.

In answer, a ready reel of New York movies popped into my mind. What did those people do? Walk dogs? Go to bars? Join a writer's group? Dog walking was a solitary thing, though, and judging by all the people I passed on the street with caps and jackets advertising various kennels, the leashes of half a dozen dogs straining in their hands, it had become a corporate thing, as well. Bars and writer's groups sounded great in films but I was no movie star, I had no charisma or even the ability to make small talk—I was shy, how would I ever meet people? What would we ever have in common? None of these things seemed to fit my reality. Sure, that's what they did on *Friends* and *Seinfeld*—there was always a ready-made support group for the people on television that moved to the city. But when I looked at the flood of faces on the sidewalks, pouring out of subway stations, moving with determination, a crowd of hundreds and thousands with each individual going their separate way, I couldn't imagine finding one person who would walk the same path as me, let alone a great crowd of them, who would conveniently all live in the same building as me, on the same *floor*, where we lived companionably with unlocked doors and shared refrigerators.

I wasn't the material for New York City. This city would chew me up and spit me out, as the saying went. I was fit only for horses and barns, throwing hay bales and wiping out noses, a nanny and a trainer to thousand-pound beasts. I could wish to be someone else, but it wouldn't matter. I looked around the streets with longing. It only made me wish for them more. It was like looking over at the cool table in middle school. Why didn't they *like* me?

I turned left at Central Park West and kept walking north, past the huge apartment houses that overlooked the park. I found myself high in the eighties as the early winter dusk began to fall, and when I sniffed the air I caught a scent of home, and so I turned and walked the long block and a half down to where the Claremont Riding Academy was hidden on the side street, with the smells of hay and ammonia wafting down from the open windows of the second story stalls.

I'd seen the odd stable before, and it had made all the equestrian magazines when the owner announced that the stables would be closed permanently, so I knew that I'd caught something fleeting and soon to disappear by getting in this surprise visit: the horses would go to new homes off the island, as the last public riding stable in Manhattan disappeared into a sea of luxury condominiums. It wasn't especially heartbreaking for me to think of the horses going to farms with turn-outs, to normal lives where they didn't have to ride a cargo elevator to the first floor arena, which didn't seem much larger than a twenty-meter circle, or walk through city traffic to get to the park's Bridle Path, overrun as it was with joggers, relentlessly pounding through woodland reveries with their earbuds firmly lodged and their iPods set to shuffle. But it was hard on the kids. Imagine living in a town where you could do anything you wanted, learn anything you were interested in—*except* ride horses. And if you couldn't ride horses, what else mattered? It was a gap that couldn't be filled. I kept questioning that, and I kept coming up with the same answer every time.

There was a riding lesson going on and the arena doors were propped open. I peered inside and watched a middle-aged woman in full-seat breeches and custom dress boots riding a flat-backed gelding with his head in the air. He was a good-looking Thoroughbred who had been around the block a few times, with bumpy cannon bones that had seen many splints and the waterfall pattern of pin-fire scars down his forelegs. He had a patient look to his eyes, as if he knew that his life was ridiculous, but that there was hay waiting in his stall if he was just nice to this rider. I adored him instantly.

"Ask him to put his head down and move nicely for you!" the instructor called.

The rider see-sawed at the reins, pulling back and forth on either side of his mouth, and ground at his back with her crotch, mistaking it for her seat bones, and the gelding obliged her conflicting directions by putting his head still higher, his mouth gaping open, his ears back and listening to her, waiting for a signal that made some sort of sense. The instructor called for her to lower her hands and she called back, "I can't, he'll run away!" and I felt a sense of tragedy that she thought she could be run away with on the lower floor of this weird New York City apartment house, on a Thoroughbred who had probably once been in his element on a mile-long oval, deep in soft sandy loam, with his rider's hands high on his neck, pressing into the mane, asking him for more, more, and still more. . .

He had left behind the training farm and the racetrack and had come to live in the city. If he could live as a rural transplant in the city, maybe I could, too. And if he hated it, maybe I would, too. That horse held the key. I felt like he was the only being in the world I could find to ask, and he wouldn't be able to answer me. The rider brought him to a choppy, off-balance halt and he stood, splay-legged and awkward as a foal, in the center of the little arena. He saw me, a shadow in the doorway against the just-lit streetlights, and his ears pricked with interest.

If I could get close to him, just lean up against him, he would tell me if he was happy or not. I just knew it. I edged closer to the line where the sand of the riding arena spilled onto the concrete of the sidewalk.

But the Thoroughbred wasn't the only one watching me. I turned away as the riding instructor noticed my non-paying presence and gave me an evil glare. I was being cast out of the garden. The street was deserted, the sky above lighting orange as the low clouds reflected the streetlights back down at the city. The commercial streets ahead seemed unnecessarily bright and loud. I wanted to stay here in the dark street with the smell of ammonia and alfalfa drifting down to me from the steamed-up windows above, but all at once the cold, and the long day, and all my mental turmoil caught up with me, and I realized that I was shivering, completely exhausted, *and* had a dinner date in three hours, which seemed unreasonably late, with a sixty-eight-year old man who would be sporting both a tweed cap and a brass-capped walking stick.

And then, once again, it started to snow. . . heavier this time, sticking to my new fleece cap and the shoulders of my new black peacoat.

I started towards Broadway so that I could look for a train station.

Ten
Escape

Jim Tilden swept off his flat tweed cap and gave me a flamboyant bow as I came up the steps of the vast, airy restaurant in Union Square. His cane swung out to one side and knocked the elbow of a passing busboy, who responded with a muttered Spanish curse and a flick of the greasy towel sticking out of his back pocket. Tilden, ever a gentleman, did not deign to notice the discomfiture of the back-of-the-house help. He merely smiled, showing gleaming dentures, and offered a hand to escort me through the multiple doors of the New York building in winter lock-down.

"My dear!" he said gallantly. "It has been far too long! I wish you had convinced old Alex to come with you, but I suppose there is no tearing him away from his young stock in the springtime!"

"No," I agreed weakly, reflecting that it was going to be awkward to be spoken about in the third person this way. No one called Alexander "Alex" anymore, not just in deference to me, perhaps, because he'd told me that he'd outgrown the name years before. But I imagine for a lot of his truly old friends, I was the driving reason why his boyhood nickname had been abandoned. Nice of him, really. I hadn't thought about it much before, but he must have insisted to his circle that they not refer to him as "Alex" anymore, and of course Tilden would not have listened. . . Tilden never listened to anyone but himself.

"Now my dear, I know you must be absolutely freezing, but come along this way, for I've persuaded the maitre'd to put us in this cozy corner away from those big drafty windows—right here! And let me order you a hot drink—She'll have a coffee with brandy," he confided to a waiter, winking conspiratorially, as if he was going to drop an engagement ring, or a roofie, something unexpected and unwanted, into my unasked-for drink. I would have preferred whisky to brandy, ten times over, but I had dined with Tilden before. He thought the essence of good manners was to micro-manage his guests so that they had absolutely no worries at all, presumably so that they concentrate on absorbing his startling wit and knowledge as he presented it to them without pause for breath.

He went on prattling, shaking out the leather-backed menu as if it was the morning paper, and after the waiter solemnly placed a vile cup of coffee, laced with brandy and impaled with a cinnamon stick, before me (which I knew I would have to drink, or resign myself to being hectored unmercifully) he cheerfully ordered us both salads and potatoes and steaks, and then got straight down to business.

"So Alex is having you ride the young stock! Well isn't that something! Isn't he worried about you? I remember letting my wife get on a horse back when she was alive; the beast swished his tail and she burst into tears." He laughed heartily; it was a favorite joke. I had heard it at least a dozen times, one for every meal we'd ever had together. I was fairly certain I'd also read it in a novel or two, so I doubted the story's authenticity.

Well, the brandy would come in handy, after all. "Honestly," I started, grimacing on a burning sip as it made its way down my throat. "I have been riding since I was a little girl, so it wasn't exactly a new experience for me. A lot of the barn managers and head riders in Ocala are women these days. Trainers find that women are good with the babies. We're a bit more patient than the average man."

"I'm sure, I'm sure," he said, nodding his head delightedly. "I do like to see a young woman on a horse. I do indeed. I always did say that the finest place for a woman was on the back of a horse. And you look ravishing in your habits, don't you, my dear!"

My lip curled and I hid my disgust behind my coffee cup. He wouldn't have been so—so—*forward,* to use a term from his own generation, if Alexander had been with me. His true colors were showing through—just another womanizing horse trainer, the kind that men laughingly call "old-fashioned," which basically meant that they thought they could prey on any woman on the backside and most of the well-dressed ones in the paddock and the clubhouse, as well. He was imagining me, and a whole faceless legion of large-hipped girls, clad in breeches and sitting astride racehorses. Anywhere but here—that was where I wished I was right now. I thought suddenly of Alexander and an evening with my head tipped onto his shoulder, drifting off to sleep to the laugh track of a sitcom. I missed Alexander, I realized suddenly, like a sharp pain in my stomach.

"I do remember a horse back in '58 or so, Montpelier, he would only let a woman near him. That blasted stud! Just hated men! He would as soon kill one as let one near him! I knew a little girl who rode the hunters for Lord Beringer—he was the big fellow in those parts, you know—and he said she could ride anything, when he heard the trouble we were having—"

The story gave no apparent hint of ending anytime soon, as he launched into a description of the "little girl's" attributes, most of which had very little to do with how she handled a horse and quite a lot to do with how she filled out a hacking jacket.

I made approximately two dozen mental notes over the course of the dinner to tell Alexander that Jim Tilden was a complete pig and he wasn't welcome on the farm anymore. I didn't know how well that was going to go over, and I didn't care. I was seething by the time the old man had cleaned his plate and sopped up the last of the steak sauce with a dinner roll. He'd spent more than an hour talking incessantly about nothing but the women he'd known on the backside and at the stud farms, and very little of it had anything to do with their horsemanship.

"And of course, lovely young women like yourself, my dear," he said, after the waiter had cleared our plates and mentioned something about a dessert selection, "Are such a beautiful addition to the racetrack. We love having you there!"

I watched his fingers do a little dance across the white tablecloth, heading dangerously near the hand I had resting near my water glass, and I thought, *this isn't happening.*

"And as for riding, well—I'm glad *you* don't have any idea of becoming a jockey. So many ladies think they can ride with men and we know that's just not true. Don't you know, my dear, girl jockeys are such a danger out on the racetrack? I mean they look very fetching, don't get me wrong—" His fingers touched mine; his leer deepened the wrinkles in his papery cheeks. His intentions became appallingly clear.

"I really should be getting back to the hotel," I gasped suddenly, bursting in on his chatter. "It's past ten o'clock and I have to be at Aqueduct by seven tomorrow. But thank you for dinner—it was lovely."

Tilden looked deeply dismayed. But I was just imagining—no, he couldn't. Alexander was an old friend. I wouldn't think it. But there was no mistaking the naked disappointment on his face. "Oh, no! I was so hoping—" he began, and then paused. He took my hand and I jerked it away as if his was on fire. I snatched at my purse and fumbled for the coat-check ticket buried within.

"Goodnight!" I said, more calm than I felt, and turned on my heel, rushing through the tables, which were *entirely* too close together, and slapped my ticket down at the coat-check girl. She smiled at me and started to ask how my dinner had been.

"I'm begging you to rush," I hissed at her. "I gotta get out of here before he sees which way I turn."

She must have had some experience in dates that got out of hand, whether it was from clients or personal experience, because she gave me a quick nod and rushed behind the curtain. I could hear the metal hangers shrieking angrily on the bar and then my coat was in my hands and she was nodding at me to go. I threw her a dollar and ran out the door.

It looked like an ideal place to hide. Union Square was a huge park, but any protection the barren trees in the center might have provided was negated by the glow of the low-hanging clouds and the dusting of snow on the ground. The buildings, on the other hand, were all brightly lit and wide open. Restaurants, diners, stores, I only had to take my pick and I could hide a while before I got back out on the streets.

Because, I wasn't ready to go back to the hotel yet. I wasn't ready to just go to bed and get up in the morning and go straight to the racetrack. I still wanted to know, and if I couldn't ask the horse, I'd have to find out myself —was this what I wanted? Could I forget about horses and do something valuable here? I wanted to get back the feeling I'd had while wandering the city earlier. I wanted to pretend that I lived here. I wanted to be that girl, one of the *girls*, one of the *people*, really, the bright young intellectuals who lived and worked and played here. I knew they existed—I saw them everywhere I turned. I could do it, couldn't I? I didn't have to live my whole life in stained polo shirts and mucky-hemmed jeans. Did I?

The Barnes & Noble glittered and allured from across the square. It was four stories of books and coffee. It seemed like a good enough place to start.

I shed coat and sweater and scarf in the cavernous café and sat down with a plain black coffee and a very edgy-looking literary journal. I looked around in expectation. Anytime now, I'd start chatting with interesting people about books and music and coffee and. . . other, interesting things.

But I didn't, of course. The minutes ticked by and although I tried to look very open and interesting, no one was going to walk over to me and say "What are you reading?" or whatever was an acceptable pick-up line for friends or fornication. And as for me, I wasn't going to do it either, for two specific reasons: I was very shy, first off. And, second off, the sadly evident fact that people come in groups. They come in pairs, or triplets, or quadruplets, but never alone. People who come to cafes alone sit along walls and cup their chins in their hands to keep their wandering eyes tight to the pages of their magazine. People who come to bookstores alone come because they have time to themselves and they wish to spend some nice personal time reading. Or they come to pretend that they have something to do on a night when no one has extended an invitation and the nights' TV programming proves too bleak. People who come to bookstores alone leave alone, having spoken to no one but the person who will take their money or direct them to the restroom.

I came to the bookstore alone, and I could see that I was going to leave it alone.

I was painfully aware that there were people here who would *not* be going home alone tonight. There were several groups of people my age, laughing and slapping the table, making entirely too much noise for a bookstore, but then again, I guessed this was a random stopping-off point before hitting the bars. It wasn't the *end* of the night, like a late-night visit to the Barnes & Noble in Ocala would be. It wasn't a nightcap and a little read because it was Sunday night and we could sleep in on Monday morning, so what the hell, let's live dangerously, baby, let's stay up until eleven! It was a place to meet and caffeinate before the revelries began.

I glared down at my silent phone, sitting emotionlessly on the table. It was ten thirty. I was tired. I propped my elbow on the table and my chin on my fist and gazed across the sea of tables at the giggling excited people, ready to go out and do something entirely unexpected. I thought about introducing myself to someone. "Hello, I'm Alex. I'm from Florida and I don't know anyone here and I have to be at the racetrack in eight hours to evaluate a racehorse. Can I join you?" It seemed like a good enough introduction. It ought to elicit some conversation, anyway. How many people walk up to you and announce that they make a living with racehorses? I'll bet these kids didn't even know that there *were* racehorses in New York City. I could be exotic and interesting. Or a redneck. I rubbed the back of my neck experimentally. The neck was one part of my body that got sun every day, even when the rest of me was covered up with riding gear and a hard hat. It was probably sunburnt to a deep rich scarlet which would glow like a neon light amongst all the pasty brunettes surrounding me. And then there was the idea of my accent—it was probably atrocious after years amongst the Appalachian drawls of north central Florida. When was the last time I'd heard myself speak? I bet I sounded like a coal-miner or an alligator-farmer. No, I couldn't do it.

The nearest table of bon vivants rose en masse and headed for the escalator. There were three girls and a guy, all of them around my age, all of them somehow taller and thinner and cooler than I was, even though, when I thought about it rationally, we were all wearing essentially the same uniform of tight jeans and a black sweater and a pair of leather boots. One of the girls, in fact, was wearing a ragged pair of Justin boots, the sort of short Western riding boot that barrel racing princesses wore, the sort that I wouldn't be caught dead in, whether in Ocala or Manhattan. I couldn't think of any rational reason why I thought that they were beyond my reach, that they had reached some echelon of NYC living that I could never reach, except for perhaps that when they went out the door they'd have a destination in mind, and I would just be wandering the streets.

So I did the only logical thing. No, I didn't go up and talk to them. Don't be ridiculous.

I followed them.

Eleven
Brooklyn

It was colder than ever out on the street, and there were snow flurries, improbably, swirling down from the orange sky above Union Square. I had always heard that when it was seriously cold, it couldn't snow—it got too cold to snow—but that clearly wasn't the case. Honestly, though, it could have been 32, it could have been ten below zero, it could have been 45, either way I would have been freezing. I was a Florida girl, in a sweater and a peacoat. Anyone would have been cold, but I had an unfair disadvantage. It was sixty-five at home right now. I had the weather app on the phone, crowing this information to me triumphantly. Sixty-five and breezy, to be exact. Unnaturally warm for a winter's night, with a clear sky and a waxing gibbous moon. The horses would be glowing white and inky black against the gray sea of the paddocks. I would be complaining about the moonlight and get up to draw the curtains after we turned out the light and climbed into bed together. I felt the knife twist in my stomach again, but I shook my head to deny it. I was more than that. I was more than the farm and Alexander. I was more than horses and dirt beneath my fingernails. I knew it. I knew it.

I followed the party down into the icy confines of the subway station, through the turnstiles and down the stairs, along with a flood of others, all ages, all races, all styles. We went through the tunnels and down more stairs, down and down and down, to the platform for the L train, where a collection of similarly dressed kids stood lounging on the platform. A piercing recorded voice announced that the next Brooklyn-bound train would be arriving in two minutes. I felt a leap of excitement and trepidation. Were we going to *Brooklyn?* What if I got lost? I'd wandered into Brooklyn exactly once, and I had no idea where I'd been. I remembered one of Alexander's acquaintances at Belmont once saying that he'd been brought up in a hell-hole somewhere in Brooklyn. That was all I had to go on in Brooklyn—a Banana Republic and a hell-hole. Which one would I end up in tonight?

This was such a bad idea. I shouldn't be down here, following some group of twenty-somethings into a train under the river. I had to go back to the hotel and get some sleep. I had to be up by five to get ready for the car and get to Aqueduct by seven to see the horse work. I should go back up the steps and into the night, hail a cab, and go to bed. My head very clearly told me what to do, and didn't that echo everything I'd ever been taught as a horsewoman? If you want to be in the horse business, you must be the sort of person who thinks with the head and not the heart.

The train pulled in, bright and silver and sparkling with automation, and the crowd of young people plowed in, and I plowed in amongst them.

I kept an eye on the group from Barnes & Noble that I'd decided to follow. It seemed pretty arbitrary at this point; nearly everyone in the train looked identical. The men wore tight jeans and boots and woolen coats and scarves and had beards and knitted caps. The women were the same, except that they didn't have beards. Yet. You know how that goes. But as it was, the train was pretty strictly 40-and-under; possibly 30-and-under. It was the antithesis of Florida. This was where all the young people lived. Whereas I lived with their grandparents. I could have followed anyone on this train, and chances are I would end up someplace altogether more exciting and more dangerous and almost certainly *louder* than anywhere I would end up back home, in their grandparent's neighborhood.

But I followed the first group, because I was starting to like them. The taller girl was the ringleader, but she had a nervous habit of brushing the long ends of her bangs behind her ears. She laughed at everything the other girl had to say, and she smiled coquettishly at the guy, who was so tall and lanky that he looked like an anorexic. But he smiled a lot, too. They *seemed* like nice people. Not the sort of people who would lead me to some drug-crazed warehouse party (those happened, right?) where the night would end when the police came to investigate accidental deaths from leaping off the roof (I must have seen this on the evening news once). More like the sort of people who would lead me to some fun club where we would see a cool band and have a couple of beers—and it would be really close to the subway station, so I wouldn't get lost. That was what was going to happen. I willed it to be so.

We got off the subway at a stop in Brooklyn called Bedford Avenue, along with a sea of others who had gotten on with us at Union Square, and after squeezing out of the narrow stairwell with the crowds, I nearly lost my group as they crossed the street. It must have snowed more here, because the street was wet and slushy at the corners, but it hadn't deterred the nightlife and behind the closed doors of the bars I could hear bass thumping and people shouting. The sidewalks were crammed with college-age kids and I had an idea that this was what I had been looking for, in my dream life, in my responsibility-free sitcom life in New York City, but at the moment it all looked a bit more than I had bargained for. A little darker, a little louder, a little dirtier. A hell of a lot colder. I hoped we would turn down Bedford Avenue —it was bright and relatively cheerful. But the crowds would disperse little by little at the corners, as groups turned off into the darkness of the side streets, heading off to their unknown destinations, and the quartet I had decided to follow did the same. I paused, torn, as they crossed Bedford, jumping over a puddle to get to the opposite sidewalk, and started to disappear into the murky street beyond. My head said to stay in the safety of the crowd, maybe just go home to the hotel.

My heart said to follow.

It was a dilemma.

I've had enough of my head, I thought. I've had enough of *you*, thank you very much. My heart wanted to *know*—could I be one of these careless kids, could I stay up all night and not once worry about a herd of hundreds depending on me for everything, could I just have *fun* like normal people had fun? Now or never. I went sloshing across the street, leaping the puddle in front of the sidewalk, and went on after my group of adopted besties.

We turned up a street and then down another, and I could see that my optimistic reliance on Manhattan's grid wasn't going to help me here. The streets had names, not numbers, and there was a diagonal-running one to throw the clean right angles off, and all the blocks looked alike, anyhow, with dark warehouses and fenced-off empty lots and brick tenements with cracked and peeling Victorian flourishes rotting from their front porches and window casements, and I got that panicking, tight feeling in my chest as I realized I couldn't turn back now. I'd never find my way back, and the five of us were practically alone on the uneven pavement. The crowds had thinned out until there was hardly anyone on the sidewalks at all, and the streets were eerily free of traffic. An occasional car passed, but no taxis at all. There would be no hailing of a cab, and finding a subway out here seemed out of the question. I was in pretty deep now.

Half a block ahead of me, the quartet of friends went stomping through the icing sidewalks, crossed another street, and turned down a wide, deserted avenue with a sharply cold wind whipping down it. Manhattan glittered to my right, and I realized that the only thing standing between us and the East River were a few rows of low garages with garlands of razor wire festooning their roofs. There was no time to ponder just how dangerous this neighborhood might be. Ahead of me, the trio disappeared into a warehouse, the concrete sidewalks illuminated momentarily by the yellow glow of the lights within, and then the door slammed shut and they, and the light, were gone.

A warehouse. I'd followed them all the way from Manhattan just to be left here in this industrial wasteland in the middle of the night, standing outside of a warehouse. I looked up and down the avenue, but there was no one on the street. I was utterly alone. So this is what it came down to, when you followed your heart? You ended up lost and alone on a cold street, shadowed by razor wire. I leaned back against the bricks of the warehouse and closed my eyes, overwhelmed by the unfairness of it all. Why couldn't I at least *try* a new life? Why was I completely unsuited for anything but the farm?

The bricks at my back were pulsing, I realized dimly. I opened my eyes. There was music playing in there.

Someone laughed, drunkenly, down the street and I watched a couple come skipping up the sidewalk, lurching across the pavement and jumping patches of ice. They came to the big steel door right next to me, turned the handle, and opened it wide.

Music and light spilled out of the warehouse. It wasn't someone's living room or a secret opium den, it was a huge, bright space in there, thumping with bass and a someone torturing a guitar while he wailed into a squealing microphone. There was some energetic keyboard jangling. The girl who had opened the door laughed and said, "Oh no, they sound *terrible!*"

A bouncer, a huge heavy-set bulldog of a man with tattoos darkening his neck and rings widening his earlobes so that you could look right through them, like novelty glasses, gestured unsmilingly with his hand and there was a fumbling in coat pockets for cash and IDs.

They went in, and I slipped over to catch the door. I showed my ID, smiled, and tried to look practiced at this sort of this thing. "What's the cover?"

"Eight," the bouncer grunted, and I shoved a ten in his hand, and didn't wait for change; I just went charging indoors into the racket and the glare, hoping that at least the press of bodies would translate into a little warmth.

It was exceedingly warm, actually, and I started imitating the masses around me, stripping off hat and coat and scarf and gloves and sweater in no particular order, whatever was expedient, and the coat check girl, who glowed with warmth as she presided over a few sliding clothes racks purloined from a Salvation Army, took a dollar from me and gave me a ticket from a spool. At last! Getting all those layers off felt *amazing.* Being warm *and* having freedom of motion for the first time in hours! I shook my shoulders and loosened my neck a little, feeling like a horse turned out after a hard ride, finally liberated of saddle and bridle. Time to enjoy myself. Pretend I was used to wandering dark streets and entering secret warehouse concerts late at night. Perfectly normal Thursday night out.

There were three men making a terrible sound on the stage, impressively loud despite having only a keyboard, a guitar, and a drum kit between them. What they lacked in numbers they made up for in volume, though, and the sound system thudded and crackled and squealed in protest while the singer went on screeching, his hair across his face, his plaid shirt knotted around his waist, sweat glistening on his rather scrawny chest. He wasn't exactly TV-ready, but I supposed he meant whatever he was singing, judging by the level of emotion he was throwing at it. The keyboardist was engaged in some sort of dance with his instrument, flinging his upper body up and down as he abused the keys, so intimate with it, in fact, that he didn't seem to notice that he was apparently playing a different song altogether from that of the taciturn guitarist, who stood facing the wall to his right, evidently pretending that he was alone in his bedroom and not on a makeshift stage in a warehouse decorated with. . . *oh*. That. . . that was pretty terrible.

There was a massive teddy bear head, mounted on a wooden plaque like a deer trophy, hanging on the back wall of the warehouse.

It fixated me, the teddy bear head. It was the sort of ridiculously sized teddy bear that carnies offer as the grand prize before they hand you the smallest little stuffed snake on the wall as your reward for knocking over all the milk jugs. The sort of gigantic teddy bear that inspires nightmares of being chased through echoing hallways by murderous plush animals before you wake up, screaming, and kick all of your former furry friends off the end of the bed in a horror. (Just me? Oh.) In any case, it was a *massive* teddy bear head. I couldn't take my eyes off its black glass eyes, which were staring blankly down at the bacchanalia below it.

"Scary, right?" said a voice in my ear. "It gives me nightmares every time I come here."

I turned and saw a smiling man standing next to me, his face disconcertingly close. Of course, he'd practically had to shout directly into my ear canal for me to hear anything over the tinnitus trio's heroic efforts to deafen us all. Still, I wasn't used to having a stranger kissing-distance when I made first eye contact.

His smile widened into a grin. "New here?"

I nodded, smiling with a little effort. No use pretending—I'd been giving that teddy bear trophy the full tourist treatment: undivided, rapt attention that I would never have afforded the Chrysler Building or the Statue of Liberty.

"Too loud on the floor. Come on, I'll show you the best spot," he said in my ear, and started to push through the crowd. I followed, not altogether certain that he wasn't going to lead me out the back door and into the dark alley behind, where he would probably kill me and chop me up in little pieces. I mean, that happened to girls like me, didn't it? Girls who wandered off to places where they didn't belong? Whole television networks were devoted to this exact situation.

At the back of the room, close to where the teddy bear was mounted above us all, surveying the scene like a plush god of Hell, there was a patio and balcony of sorts constructed. It would have been the pride and joy of a trailer-park resident, a little someplace to put the grill and maybe the spare sofa, except that this one was indoors and raised high enough that you could stand beneath it. He led me beneath it, past a few couples who were engaged in rapturous make-out sessions on the wooden benches built into the back wall, and then up a set of truly alarming stairs, made, as best as I could tell, out of remnants from lumber yards and things found in aforementioned dark alleys. I hesitated, but no—I was following my heart and not my head. The wood sagged gently beneath my boots with every step. It would be a flashy headline: *Gallop girl dies in warehouse party patio collapse.*

Up top, just under the murky tin ceiling, the air was incredibly hot. There were round cafe tables scattered around the mezzanine, and little groups sat comfortably, drinks on the tables before them, looking down at the performance, which was muted by nearly half, since we were now higher than the speakers. The men were in t-shirts and the women were in various states of semi-undress, no one wearing anything more concealing than a camisole, giving the whole place a bizarre feeling of summer garden party.

"Nice, right?" the young guy smiled at me, and I thought that he smiled rather excessively for someone who didn't know me at all. I could guess that he was trying to pick me up. I just wasn't sure why. Did I look easy? Simple, lost, confused? Probably all of these things. The only guys in Ocala who tried to pick me up were dudes in cowboy hats at the feed store, and that really wasn't my scene. I would have been all kinds of flattered by this guy, who looked like he'd walked out of a magazine cover in his tight jeans, red and white plaid shirt, and horn-rimmed nerd glasses. I *would* have been. Except I was pretty sure that this was less about my looks, and more about my dazed look, which made me easy prey for a man on the prowl.

But still, there was something to be said for being someone's focus, the more I thought about it. I decided to let it go where it would.

"Want to sit and have a drink?" he asked, all puppy-dog friendly. "I have a table right over there." He gestured to a table in the corner, piled with coats and sweaters in a "this-seat-is-saved" kind of message.

"Sure, thanks," I said. Did I add a syllable to 'thanks'? I was once again feeling nervous that I might have unknowingly developed a southern accent.

"What can I get you?"

"Oh—whatever you're having," I said amiably, not ready to be troubled with making a decision, and settled into the metal chair.

He came back with two caramel-brown shots and two big cans of Rolling Rock. "The specialty here," he explained. "Too good to pass up. But if you don't want the shot—"

I'm a *racetracker*. But bless him for thinking I could be otherwise. I tossed it back and smiled, setting the glass down.

His eyebrows went up. He turned back his own glass. "So I'm Ryan," he said. "Twenty-four, graphic designer, bass player in really horrible band, live in Greenpoint. That's me. You?"

I grinned, fortified already by the whiskey. It was warm and fierce and utterly delicious in my mouth and throat and chest. "Alex, twenty-five, horse trainer, live in Florida."

"Horse trainer? You're kidding!"

"Oh no," I said, popping open the can of Rolling Rock. I pointed at the horse. Whiskey loosened my tongue immediately. "Always a favorite of mine, just because of this little guy." I tickled the white horse's chin, and Ryan grinned. "So anyway, yeah, I train racehorses. I'm assistant manager on a two hundred-acre farm in Ocala."

"Whoa," he said. "That's pretty amazing. I mean— wow. You get on racehorses? You're like a jockey? That's unreal."

I smiled, pleased with the response. "Like a jockey, but I don't do the racing. I let the *real* little guys do that."

"Unbelievable."

"Being a graphic designer sounds great!" I said sincerely. "I think I'd love that."

"Oh." He shook his head. "Oh, everyone does that. Everyone here is either a graphics designer or an app designer or a social media expert. Or a writer."

"I'd like to be a writer," I said, suddenly wistful. "I'd like to live here and be a writer."

He looked doubtful. "You'd rather live here and be a writer than ride racehorses?"

"You think that's no good?"

"Oh, just," he looked around. "There's no shortage of writers."

The trio of poorly matched singers announced the end of their set with a flamboyant *"Thankyougoodnight!"* and the audience cheered, whether from admiration or relief, I couldn't have said, and then it was suddenly quiet in the little warehouse. Despite the buzz of conversations and the clinking of glasses in the bar, it felt absolutely silent after the din of the band was silenced. Everyone lowered their voices a little, and then the truly drunk amongst the drinkers stood out, still shouting as if there was amplified music in the room. I smiled down at the crowd below, but I was suddenly confused about my place here, wondering if Ryan wasn't right after all. Maybe this could never be more than a silly vacation, an idle dream. Maybe I wouldn't want it any other way.

"Hey, there's my friend Samuel," Ryan said suddenly, and he shouted across the porch. "Samuel! Samuel! Come meet this girl!"

Samuel was a tall lumberjack sort of fellow who didn't look like he had touched a razor to his face since he escaped from the pack of bears who had raised him deep in the forests of Canada. He grinned knowingly at Ryan and offered me a paw to shake. "How do you do?" he said in a parody of good manners. I laughed. The whiskey and beer were doing their job. Dinner had been a long time ago.

I put on my most terrible southern accent for the occasion. "Well bless me but the manners in New York City have to be *seen* to be *bay-leeved!*" I brayed. "Aren't you a *sweetheart?*"

The lumberjack bear laughed. "Ryan, where did you find this one? Where are you from?"

"She's a *racehorse* trainer from *Florida,*" Ryan said proudly, as if he had constructed me from glue and popsicle sticks.

"You're kidding! What are you doing here?"

"I have to go look at a horse at Aqueduct in—" I looked at my phone. "About six hours."

"What's Aqueduct?" Ryan enquired. "Is that like, a riding stable or something? Is that that crazy place by Prospect Park? They ride horses in the streets, man—"

"It's a *racetrack,*" I gasped, genuinely horrified. "You don't know there are racetracks here?"

"For *horses?*" Samuel asked, looking confused. "For horses, not cars." He shook his head. That didn't sound right to him.

"There aren't any car racetracks here," Ryan chided him.

"So you know *that.*" I was pissed.

"Hey, hey, come on, you know neither of us are *from* here. I'm from St. Louis and Samuel is from Cleveland."

Samuel laughed. "No one in this room is *from* here."

I sighed. "Well, New York City is the heart of horse racing. The term 'The Big Apple' comes from horse racing, did you know that?"

They shook their heads and waited for an explanation.

"It was the big treat—coming to the New York racetracks was the prize grooms looked forward to all year. Anyway, there is a racetrack in Queens and another one just over the border in Long Island. I'm going to the one in Queens to look at a horse for our farm."

They didn't ask about the "our" and I didn't enlighten them. No need to lose my audience just because I happened to be in a committed relationship with Alexander. He wasn't here and—I took a deep swig of Rolling Rock to quell the sudden lump in my throat. Damn, I missed him. Damn and damn and damn. I could feel my little New York fantasy dissolving around me.

And yet here I sat! Surrounded by interested men in a nightclub! Okay, nightclub wasn't the right word for this warehouse somewhere in Brooklyn, but, even so, both of these guys seemed quite fascinated by me, and I liked it.

Samuel had gone across the porch and was dragging two more people over. I recognized the taller girl from the group I had followed here from Manhattan. She clung to the hand of a skinny redheaded guy, wearing the universal uniform of plaid shirt and tight jeans, wisps of scraggly beard clinging to his chin and cheeks. "Dude, that bear is *messed* up," he was drawling as he came up.

"Amy," Samuel said, "This girl trains *racehorses*. How crazy is that?"

She smiled and looked me over without a flicker of recognition—although it would have taken superpowers to place me as the woolly Eskimo I had resembled out on the cold streets—and held out a bony hand to shake. "I'm Amy." She paused. "And this is Skyler." The redhead gave me an arresting look with startlingly pale blue eyes, and then his eyes wandered back towards the teddy bear, who overlooked the proceedings with blank detachment.

"Bear's creeping me out," he murmured. Amy shook her head.

"Don't mind him. Tell me about horses." She sat down across from me and looked expectant. Amy was used to being in charge.

So I told them. I told the group about riding racehorses at sunrise, about pulling on a foal's legs as a mare strained in a midnight foaling, about driving a truck and hauling a rig, about how hard the ground was when you hit it, and about putting your face close to your horse's ears when he was galloping flat-out, about the judicious use of the whip and how it could be used as an "ask" instead of a punishment, about the feeling of fog droplets on your bare arm in the mornings, about the heat of the afternoons and creeping indoors to sleep through a thunderstorm.

And then in the midst of describing all the beauty of my life, hauntingly gorgeous with the nostalgic tinge of miles and miles of separation, my phone buzzed, and I pulled it out and looked at the text message from Alexander, that said "Can't sleep alone. I miss you, little love," and I had to wipe a few stray tears away.

"And what do you think of Brooklyn, then?" Amy demanded.

What did I think of Brooklyn? The dark streets, the hulking warehouses, the biting cold, the one brief sparkling street full of kids back at the subway, the glass-eyed teddy bear gazing out over us all with regal disinterest? The crowd of people gathered around me at a little metal cafe table, on a plywood balcony in a glorified garage with a band playing on the stage below us, their urgent questions and unqualified interest in *me?* I hadn't really seen Brooklyn, but Brooklyn I'd seen sure seemed to like me. "I could live here," I said experimentally, even though I knew I couldn't. The stories I had just told them ensured that. I was ensnared by my own life.

"And do what?" Amy asked. She seemed fiercely practical. "There aren't any horses here."

"There's the racetrack," I pointed out. "I could go and work there."

"Well, that's Queens, though," Ryan said, and everyone nodded in agreement. Queens was not at all the same thing. "And you said it's all really early mornings. That doesn't sound very fun."

"Wouldn't you miss the farm and the fields and all the space?" a girl asked, leaning over Amy's shoulder. "And Alexander?"

"Yeah, what about Alexander?" Amy asked expectantly. "You'd give up all that and your relationship and everything?"

"Guys, guys," Ryan said. "That's so none of our business."

"It kind of is," Amy retorted. "Now that we're all interested in her life." She smiled at me. "You're our new favorite soap opera, sweetie."

Twelve
Religion and politics

"So what you're saying," Ryan said to me, setting down his beer on the bar and raising a hand to the bartender for another, "Is that you think you could be a writer if only you left everything you ever knew and your boyfriend of several years and moved here."

We were sitting at the bar of a very loud, very small club somewhere near an elevated expressway in another part of Williamsburg. I had four hours until my appointment at Aqueduct, another hour before the bars closed. I was in a weird haze, not quite sober and not quite drunk, somewhere closer, it must be admitted, to regaining the buzz I'd acquired at the warehouse back by the river. "You have a way of making it sound foolish," I said morosely, studying the dying suds in my beer. "And selfish."

"Well, it is!" he laughed. "Forgive me for saying it, but it's both. Listen—everyone you met tonight is an artist or a writer or a musician. We're all practically the same *person*. We eat the same food and wear the same clothes and listen to the same music. We read the same books. The bookmarks on our computers are all the same, for god's sake. And let me tell you something else—none of us are from here, and none of us, or very few of us, will stay here. Because after a while, it's very tiring being the same as everyone else."

I thought I could commiserate with that. "It's the same in Ocala, though!" I protested. "We're all horsemen, all we ever think about are horses, we go to Starbucks and there are pictures of horses on the walls, we go to the bookstore and look at books about horses—"

"You don't, though, do you?" he asked. "You read other stuff. You think about other stuff. That makes you different."

"No one really knows that."

"Well," he said, sitting back and smiling at me. "That's on you. But I bet someone knows."

"Alexander."

"He must know, or he wouldn't choose to spend all his time with a girl twenty years his junior, am I right? I mean, a sexual attraction is one thing. But he spends all his time with you. He must like your brain, too, Alex."

I let my mind run back over the things we talked about. Just horses, right? All I could remember was horses, horses, horses. But no. Wait. Just two days ago, but a million years ago, in the broodmare barn, we'd talked about the last couple of books we'd read, while I held the tail of a pregnant mare over my shoulder to keep it out of the vet's way while she leaned, shoulder-deep, into the mare to check the foal's progress. Last Sunday, we'd read the paper and drank coffee and sat in a deep, content silence. A few days before, he'd asked if I wanted to join the museum of art's membership program, so that we could attend their parties and talks. We hadn't been close since Saltpeter had died, true, but we were still a couple, still interested in the same things, not all of which had four legs and swishy tails. Somehow, I'd thought everything in our lives had dwindled down to horses. I'd confused things. I'd rewritten our history, and left whole chapters out. "I thought they were the beginning and end of everything. . ." I said slowly. "I thought we didn't have *anything* but horses. . ."

"Maybe they are the beginning and end of everything," Ryan suggested. "But there's something else in the middle."

We thought about this, a matched pair, chins on fists, gazing down at the water-stained surface of the bar. The din around us was nothing but a buzzing in my ears, all the shouting voices and the roaring jukebox in the background blurring together into an incomprehensible mess. There was no turning it off, here in this city. It was noisy in the bars, it was noisy in the streets, it was noisy in the empty hotel room, the sounds from the sidewalk and the pavement floating up and intruding through the glass and bricks. It was probably noisy in Ryan's apartment. There was never a perfect silence.

There was something to be said for music and conversation when you wanted it, and silence when you didn't.

I closed my eyes.

I had my forehead pressed against Saltpeter's skull, the swirling patterns of his white and gray hairs a spiral between his dark eyes, and his forelock parted on either side of my head and tickled my ears, and I could feel his warm, moist breath on my hands, cupped beneath his chin and holding him gently, gently, so that he wouldn't get claustrophobic, overwhelmed by human affection, and would just share that simple, silent moment with me. Horses only spoke when absolutely necessary, and wild horses would never speak at all; sound would give away their location, and horses only want to be known to their kin. A barn full of confident, foolish young horses was alive and rowdy with whinnies and neighs; a horse alone with a human was often quiet, protecting them both from the outside world.

The noise was unbearable; there was safety in silence.

Saltpeter was dead, dead, dead.

I opened my eyes and the sound assailed me, voices defining themselves again, the songs pulling back to cover their own sonic territory; the clink of glasses and the sliding of a bar stool across the floor added themselves to the general din.

My friends were dead and I was alone in this noisy place.

Ryan had been reflecting on mortality, too.

"Hey," Ryan said suddenly. "People eat horses, don't they? Why don't you use their bodies?"

"Oh, god, Ryan. Gross." I took a drink; the spell was broken.

"It's a reasonable question—*wouldn't* you eat a horse?"

"Of course not, Ryan, Jesus—how could you ask me such a thing?" My darling Saltpeter, my gleaming Red Erin, hadn't they earned a dignified rest? I thought of their dark eyes watching me, of my hands grasping their coarse manes. Saltpeter's gentle nips if you were standing close by but not paying him your full and undivided attention; Red Erin's insistence on licking my hand like an oversized Golden Retriever.

"Look at it like this," he said, looking extremely put-upon for having to explain himself. "Horses die. They have tons of meat on them. People are starving. What would be wrong with eating them?"

I slammed my beer glass down on the bar, hard enough to attract the disapproving glare of the bartender. *Whatever.* I had tipped over the line again, grown too drunk to care. "Ryan, you're absolutely right. Horses die. Would you like to hear *how* they die?"

Ryan looked pale.

"First, you notice that they seem a little off, so you give them some bute—that's like aspirin, only it's toxic to humans—to see if it's just a little ache, not a big deal.

Then you take them off of the bute and they seem fine, so you take them out and give them a little work out. The next day they're worse. You have the vet out, the vet takes X-rays, finds a *fracture*. Not a huge fracture, but a fracture. Or maybe he just laid down in his stall wrong and busted his leg that way. Horses are too damn fragile." I paused long enough to polish off the beer. "Yo! Another beer!" I shouted. The bartender looked aggrieved. The racetracker in me was in full control of the situation now.

"So he puts him down. Right there in front of you, he injects the horse and that's that. He's dead."

The beer was put down in front of me and I took a swig to sustain my anger. The dead were crowding around me; their stories were vivid in my mind.

"*Or*, you find a bone chip, not a fracture, and you end up doing surgery. You put the horse under and do arthroscopic surgery. This takes some heavy-duty sedatives and of course after that you have to load the horse up with antibiotics. During this time his leg is in a cast and he's stuck in a stall. He isn't getting to walk around enough, which means the blood flow to his hooves is compromised, because the hooves act as four additional heartbeats—did you know that? Most people don't—and he ends up lying on his side, groaning with pain like a human, because the *insides* of his hooves are inflamed and pressing against the hard outer walls.

"And so, after lots more drugs and sedatives and painkillers, all of which are toxic to humans in varying amounts, the horse is finally euthanized, to spare him further pain, and his body is dragged out by a tractor and burned, because if you bury that *bio-hazard* of a body in your flooded fields, you will contaminate your groundwater. And that, Ryan, is how horses die. Still wanna eat one?" I craned my neck around to glare at him.

Ryan looked down at the water-rings on the warped bar. Then he looked up at me. "Who died?"

I sighed. "Two horses. One last year, one a few weeks ago. I guess you can say 'just another horse.' That's what you're supposed to say. Because they die. But I loved them. I love them all." I sniffed. All the alcohol was making me emotional. "I hated seeing his body burn. We couldn't do that with the horse a few weeks ago. We took the risk and buried him in an upper field. . . the water table was lower. But still—he was alive and happy and then he just *wasn't.* "

"But you *had* to put him to sleep. . . right?"

"Of course!" I said firmly. "There was no other option—he was in pain and he wasn't going to get better. I just hate these stupid decisions—you have to make way too many of them. They're *hard.* They break your heart, and you have to just take it. A person has to think with the head and not the heart, in horses. . ." I trailed off and examined the beer before me. "It's hard. Not everyone can do it. Not all the time."

Ryan leaned over and put his hand on mine. I looked at it, so pale and alien against my dark calloused skin. He worked on computers all day while I was out wrestling with horses; he sat in bars all night while I fell asleep over supper at eight o'clock at night. But I had great loves, such great loves, in my life.

"You can't live without horses," he said to me, and I nodded.

Thirteen
Aqueduct

The wind was absolutely bone-chilling at Aqueduct. I shrank back against the cushions of the town car's backseat, not willing to get out of the heated sanctuary, but there was nothing for it, the security guard was leaning down chivalrously, a hand extended to help me out, and I had to bite my chapped lips and go out into that gale. I was sure there would be a blizzard at any moment —with this wind, with this cold!—and I would be stuck in it, stuck in some tack room hovering over a space heater with a couple of grooms and some hunchbacked retired jockeys and a leering, wise-cracking trainer making awful jokes about how I was the only female for miles and men had needs. I'd already paid the driver and he was looking back at me in the rearview mirror. His radio crackled. He was late for a pick-up at the airport. He lifted an eyebrow at me, and I sighed and took the security guard's hand.

"My dear lady," the security guard said in a strange accent, something between New York and Mexico City, "I am so happy to have you here at Aqueduct."

I stared at him, unprepared for this speech, while he continued to clasp my hand and gaze into my eyes. He looked like a parody of a state trooper, in a dark green polyester guard's uniform with a New York Racing Association badge and a wide-brimmed cowboy hat, and a great bushy mustache bristling over his mouth, possibly modeled on the inimitable Sam Elliot's.

"My name is Romeo," he continued, "Because I have great love for all women."

I looked at his chest—anything to avoid eye contact, which he was strenuously attempting to hold—and saw that his embroidered nametag did, indeed, say, "Romeo."

Oh, dear god, Romeo, I hope that there is something lost in translation here.

"You are here to see Mr. Figaro, yes?" Romeo said solicitously. "Come, I escort you to him. Come, come." He tucked my hand more securely in his, holding it high before his chest, and led me across the slushy parking lot, taking me in elaborate zig-zags to avoid patches of ice in the rutted asphalt. If I hadn't been so miserably cold, huddled up within my two horsey sweaters (the only two sweaters I owned that weren't *completely* turned over to the vagaries of broodmares and foals and other destructive equine beings) and my inadequate winter coat, I would have shaken him off, regained a little pride, but it was all I could do to put one foot in front of the other and keep my eyes open in that bitterly cold wind.

We climbed up a flight of stairs that led up a berm from the parking lot, and there, past an empty guard shack with a fluorescent light flashing on and off like lightning within, was the great asphalt expanse of the stabling area, a quarter mile in either direction of flat-roofed, 1950s era stables, looking like something NASA might have built at Kennedy Space Center in the years before the moonshots, with louvered windows pulled tight against the arctic cold. The windows were pitted with baseball-sized holes, as if there were an unfortunate profusion of home-runs from parking lot pick-up games, and pigeons flew in and out of the barns as freely as swallows would, in a more conventional horse barn, in a more conventional place than New York City.

I was looking curiously at the first barn we passed, with huge rusting steel doors painted with Aqueduct's logo, a straining horsehead emerging from a capital letter "A", when the earsplitting sound of a screaming engine pierced the morning and I looked up to see an Emirates jet, its red underbelly and white letters reading "Fly Emirates" picked out orange in the rising sunlight, buzzing the racetrack from a dangerously low height. It sailed over our heads and on across the street and over the huddled brick houses beyond, disappearing behind the chimneys and leafless trees of the neighborhood that sat sandwiched between the racetrack, the expressway, and, apparently, the airport.

"Oh my god!" I gasped, after the jet had passed enough for human speech to be audible once again. "What the hell was that?"

"That's normal, my lady," Romeo laughed, squeezing my icy fingers. "We right next to JFK. We in the flight path. You can walk from here to the airport. You didn't see us waving up at you when you flew in?"

"I saw the beach," I said. "Must have been a different flight pattern." I'd leaned against the window and seen the fog lift just enough to show me New York's very strange beach, lined with what looked suspiciously tall brick project housing. It didn't even remotely resemble beach front real estate in Florida. They definitely treated their waterfront differently in New York City, I could say that much. Although with this stabbing, horrible wind, I couldn't see how beachfront property would be very desirable here. I thought sadly of white sand and blue water, palm trees and hammocks and drinks with umbrellas. I wanted Alexander back. I wanted my life back, muck and mud and bruises and all. I was going to look at this horse and get the hell out.

"Oh, too bad! Maybe you see us when you leave!" He continued to chuckle in a creepy kind of way and went on leading me past identical barns. I was impatient to get to Figaro's. There had to be an office and a space heater. Maybe some coffee? Or maybe—I pulled my hat up a little to ease the pressure on my skull—maybe something stronger.

Barns in winter are never warm places, even though four walls and a roof would offer some supposed protection from the weather, and the Aqueduct barns rattled and wailed with age and drafts. Romeo pulled back a sliding door, and I found myself in the rutted sandy shedrow of a training barn, with dilapidated concrete block stalls running back to back and horses leaning out over stall webbings, pulling at thickly packed haynets that hung from rings outside their stall doors. I stepped back almost immediately to let a shaggy dark horse go jogging past, his mouth foaming white against the bit, his chin nearly pulled back to his chest with the upper-body strength of the straining rider atop him, a wiry little Latino man who found the time to give me a leering grin as he rode around the corner, the horse's legs swinging out on the turn like a dancer's.

"Two more times, Marco!" A small man emerged from a door a short distance down the shed, across from the rows of stalls, and held up a hand in greeting. "Romeo, what did you bring us? Our little Florida bird? You must be Alex! I'm Dickie Figaro. Call me Dickie."

Oh, dear god. "Morning, Dickie," I said, walking along the hard-packed ground close to the shedrow wall. "So nice to meet you." We shook gloved hands and nodded fleece-capped heads and then he walked me down to a stall where a dark horse was single-mindedly destroying a haynet full of hay. *Destroying* it. He would rip out chunks with bared teeth, like a wolf tearing the flesh of its prey, and slam his head into the net if it wasn't positioned exactly as he wanted. He flung his head up and down at us, nodding insanely, before he went back to the hay. He certainly had a lot of stage presence.

"This is The Tiger Prince," Dickie said proudly, and I could hear the capital letters in the horse's title.

"*The* Tiger Prince?" I asked, admiring what I could see of the horse. He was clipped and in gleaming good health, but his body was hidden beneath a brown and blue plaid Baker blanket.

"Yup," Dickie said. "Tiger Tiger out of Erin's Princess. Good New York mare but ended up in Florida. You must have heard of her."

"Of course." He didn't need to play games, I thought impatiently. Anyone with Google could have figured out within two minutes that Alexander and I had owned this colt's half-brother. He had to know why we were so interested. Of course we'd heard of Erin's Princess.

The horse eyed me while he continued to attack his haynet, interested, but not interested enough to give up on the hay. Or, maybe, showing off. The good ones have panache. They *want* to be stars. The Tiger Prince was certainly giving me that rock star vibe: an impression of royalty combined with a high sense of drama. I laid a hand on his glossy neck, so dark it was nearly black, and was rewarded with his full attention. Ears pricked, he leaned over, delicately gave my gloved hands a deep sniff, and then snorted. Hard. The kind of horse snort that leaves little black sticky souvenirs all over you. The kind of horse snort that can destroy white clothes forever. I looked down at my new black coat and brushed at the specks of snot, destined to cling to the woolen knit until the end of time. Barn coat, just like that. "You," I told the horse, "are a horrible, bad boy."

He went back to his hay. I was already in love.

"Well," I said to Dickie, who was looking embarrassed about the nonchalant destruction of my clothes. "He seems nice enough as a person. Can you get someone down here to tack him up and take him out?"

A groom, idling in the tack room door over a paper cup of coffee, was dispatched to get the horse ready. He came back out with saddle, bridle, yoke, and blankets over his arm and set it all on the stall webbing. He turned his back to find a brush, which gave The Tiger Prince just enough time to grab hold of the saddle and flip it off the webbing, falling with a crash to the straw at his hooves. The groom cursed and looked at me, turned the curse into a laugh, and shook his head, before going into the stall to tie the horse up to the wall, out of reach of the tack, before he picked up the toppled saddlery.

I watched his interaction with the groom carefully, just to confirm my initial impression of his temperament. A clever joker, that's what The Tiger Prince was. He was relatively quiet and polite, but little touches of mischief gave him away. He watched the groom carefully, one eye rolled back to see what the poor guy was up to, and took little playful snatches in his direction whenever the groom was in biting distance. He could have bit him a dozen times over, but he never actually reached all the way—he was just looking for a game.

It was the same with his hind end—he wasn't above slapping the groom with his tail from time to time, or picking up his hind leg and giving it a little shake as if he was considering giving the groom a good kick.

I felt a surge of nostalgia for Red Erin, watching this dark brother of his. They were very like. Red Erin had been a burnished red chestnut, sure, while this horse was a dark bay, nearly black, but there—there was the same little anklet of white on the right hind, with little ermine spots patching his heel, and there was the same white dot on his nose, just large enough for a chiding index finger —or a kiss. And the expression in his eyes was the same —a brainy troublemaker, my favorite sort of horse. I was such a sucker for the clever ones.

"How long has he been at the track?" I asked Figaro. It looked like he could use some time out in a paddock. His brain was stuck on having fun, not working. Red Erin always needed lots of time outside. Figaro got his horses cheap because they had problems, and I suspected his lack of attention might be the reason for the colt's fall from grace.

"Oh, since January," Figaro said, shrugging. "Not long. He was up in Saratoga as a yearling, though."

"So he hasn't been outside much in a while?"

"Oh, no," he said. "They got too much snow up there. Got an indoor track for starting the babies on, you know, but it snows so damn much you can't open the barn doors in the middle of winter. This guy hasn't been turned out in months, if that's what you're getting at."

I smiled. "That's exactly what I'm getting at, Dickie. You see it too?"

"Oh yeah, I see it." He shrugged. "This is the way it is. They live here, they stay inside. They get all pent up and they win races that way, though, you know? Sometimes you shut the stall door for two-three days and don't let them see the outside world none at all. They come out and win that race like their tail is on fire. It's a good trick!" He laughed, and I smiled, but inside I was seething. That was no way to treat a horse, a herd animal who was terrified of being alone. I knew it was common, but I didn't have to like it.

The horse seemed nice enough, though, and if his little naughty nips and kicks were nothing more than pent-up energy, I could live with that. As a rule, I didn't like anyone who wasn't nice in the barn; I suppose it is a holdover from riding as a child, when it didn't matter how nicely a horse moved if he couldn't be trusted in a barn full of children. Some racehorse trainers will put up with any amount of bad behavior—some think it to be an encouraging sign that a horse is ready to win—but I demanded respect and good manners, and so did Alexander. I nodded when the horse was brought around to the front of the stall, fully tacked, and moved to the safety of the tack room door while Figaro opened up the stall webbing to let them out.

He squealed a little as his hooves hit the soft sand of the shedrow's rutted track, and threatened to kick out, crowhopping ever so slightly, but if that was the worst behavior a cooped-up, hyper-fit racehorse gave when he left his stall in the morning, we should all be so lucky. Red Erin hadn't been above the occasional buck. And Saltpeter used to rear unless you popped him on the neck with the stick, just to remind him that you had it, and you weren't afraid to use it.

Saltpeter. Red Erin. It was getting depressing, comparing this horse to my dead favorites. I was suddenly afraid I would fall in love this horse and then lose him as well. The groom took him down the shedrow and then they disappeared around the corner, the colt's tail swishing from side to side with each precise footfall. I sighed. He was painfully lovely, achingly perfect, and my two lost boys swelled up as a lump in my dry throat. I longed for Alexander's comforting presence, someone to lean into, someone who would have understood such love.

"And how are you enjoying New York?" Figaro asked, after he had given the rider a leg-up and we had all trooped out from the barn behind the horse. The horse went on up the path towards the gap where they entered and exited the racetrack, while we went up the steep hill to the trackside and went up the wobbly metal stairs of a trainer's viewing stand, a little wooden hut complete with a heater so formidable I started to sweat under my sweaters and coat immediately. The trainer poured me a cup of suspicious-looking coffee, to which I added several sugar packets and a glug of half-and-half from a stable bucket doubling as an ice chest.

"It's been great," I said, managing not to choke on the coffee. "I met Jim Tilden in Union Square last night and we had dinner."

"Oh, Jimmy Tilden!" Figaro said familiarly. "Quite a guy, quite a guy. But something tells me you've done more than that, missie. The kids wear sunglasses here for a reason."

I stared at him, mystified. The sun was hardly up—why would I need sunglasses?

"Your *eyes,*" he clarified. He leaned onto the counter and watched a few horses go jogging past just below us, their heads turned towards the outer rail in a bid to keep them down to a trot. They were going the "wrong way," to keep them out of the way of horses galloping along the inner rail. A set of three horses came galloping into the backstretch in a tight *v*, like a flock of geese, and overtook a slower horse cantering along on his own. They flashed past him on the inside and the slower horse went into a series of bucks, flinging himself sideways, before the rider could get him straightened out with boot and whip. Riding on the racetrack was chaotic, all these different horse and rider combinations all going about their own business, whether they were new to the track or old and experienced. I preferred the safety of our own training track, where we rode as a team. In the same direction.

Figaro wasn't ready to give up. He'd seen horses before, these were nothing new. It was more fun, I guessed, to bait the country girl. "Your eyes give you away, sweetheart. You haven't been to bed in a while."

"I think just the fact that's she's drinkin' that cawfee gives her away, Dickie!" laughed a heavy-set man with a thick local accent. "That's *rotgut,* that's what that is!"

It was true, the coffee was appalling but the headache that was threatening to settle in was even worse. Caffeine wasn't going to take care of the whole job, and I wondered if Figaro was one of those appealing souls who gave his horses Guinness—a little of the feed room stash and I'd be in business. "I met some friends in Brooklyn last night," I confirmed, and then pointed, to try and get the subject back to the colt: "Is that the horse, right there?"

Figaro looked. "Yeah, that's him. Nice trot on him."

It *was* a nice trot. It was Red Erin's trot, but even nicer. He had a lot of reach from his shoulder. Some horses trot straight up and down, picking up their knees the way a human jogs. They work harder and expend more energy that way. Some horses trot forward and back, swinging their leg from their shoulders and barely bending their knees. I love to see beautiful efficiency of motion in a horse.

He went past us, nearly right below us, with his head and neck pulled in a taut bow back towards the inner rail. The rider was standing in the stirrups to hold him back. I admired his expression: bright, curious eyes, ears pricked, and then he was past us, sweeping to cut past the open expanse of the chute where the starting gate sat, on towards the clubhouse turn.

"Watch him right there," the man in the corner laughed, his wide neck wobbling. "See that tractor? There's a sliding gate there, just a piece of PVC in the rail, and it wobbles in the wind. Everyone spooks at it. Just watch."

As the colt approached the parked tractor, he went into a plunging, sideways gallop and the rider had to work to get him under control again.

"I told yez!" the man laughed, slapping his knee. "Can't no one get past that damn gate in the wind."

Figaro smiled thinly. "They're high-strung, Pete, what else do you want?"

"I just like to watch them have their fun," Pete chortled. "Make those jocks earn their keep."

"He'll turn back at the wire and gallop around for us," Figaro told me, turning his back on Pete. "I told the jock to open him up at the three-eighths pole and then keep him going, so you'll be able to see him moving out."

"Great," I said, and went back to my coffee. I watched the horse go around the sweeping turn towards the grandstand. Beyond him, on a berm just past the grandstand, a silver subway train went rattling by. It was a strange juxtaposition of city and country—I found it hard to comprehend that I was watching a *horse* with something so quintessentially urban as a New York City subway train in the same picture. But The Tiger Prince took no notice; trains were as much a part of his life as rabbits and foxes were to my horses in Ocala. I wondered what he'd do if he actually saw a rabbit. Lose his mind, probably. Dump his rider and run for miles.

"Have a nice time last night?" Pete asked maliciously, chuckling. "I hear you kids really tear it up in Brooklyn. We did too when we was kids, but it's not the same place anymore. Not so rough."

"Well, I went to a warehouse down by the East River, to see a few bands," I said, hoping I could make it sound much more intentional and bohemian than it had actually been, "And then we went and closed down a bar near the BQE." I liked pretending to be a dangerous night-owl. I liked pretending I wasn't longing and longing for my bed right now. *Our* bed, mine and Alexander's, not the hotel room bed, or the couch in Ryan's apartment where his roommates had made me coffee and asked me about, what else, horses, until the town car arrived to cart me here. There wasn't any doubt in my mind now, after that night out, or this bitterly cold morning here amongst these rough-hewn men. I wanted to go home to Alexander, pull the curtains against the Florida sun, and stay in bed for the rest of the day.

I pulled out my phone and sent him a message, the third of the morning. "Getting ready to watch him gallop. Super nice. A lot like Red Erin. Love you."

The phone dinged before I could put it away. "Hurry home. Love you Alex."

I was impatient for the horse to gallop. I needed to hurry home.

"Where is he?"

"Standing up at the wire," Dickie said. "Look, now he's going to take him. Red helmet cover."

There was a collection of half a dozen horses standing between the clubhouse turn and the far end of the grandstand. Their riders pulled them up, made them stand still so that they could observe the other horses and the activity bustling around the backside, and then, after a few minutes, sent them off into a gallop the right way, counter-clockwise, around the track. The Tiger Prince, who had been standing like a statue at the wire, looking around at the busy track and waiting for a good gap in traffic, now was sent off into an easy canter down the center of the track. Despite the distance, I could see the ease of his motion, the gentle rhythm his head and neck made as they rocked back and forth with his gait. I liked him. A lot.

In no time he was turning onto the backstretch and made a quick clean flying lead change as he came around the turn, jumping so that his leading, more hard-working legs became his outside, right legs, saving his left legs for the turns, both for balance and for rest. He would change to his right lead once again at the top of the stretch, and those fresh legs would give him the extra leap in his step he'd need to make a bid for the win. A horse who didn't have to be constantly reminded, who knew to change his leads on turns and when he got tired in the homestretch was a very clever horse, was a winning sort of horse.

His action was low and close to the ground—he didn't waste energy picking up his legs very high. He was a very American sort of horse, very well-suited to skimming over dirt tracks, the kind of horse who would go straight to the front and run away with the race. He'd be a lovely sprinter, just as Red Erin had been. No Derby horse this, but we could run him in Florida very happily, have some fun with him, enjoy his big personality.

I pulled out my phone again and set the timer, ready to hit the button the moment the horse started really galloping. My finger dropped at the three-eighths pole, which is nearly at the head of the homestretch, when the jockey let loose and the horse exploded forward, as if he'd been standing still before instead of merely cantering. I raised my eyebrows, careful to be quiet. The heavy man in the corner was less circumspect. *"Wow,"* he said. "Dickie—that's some breeze."

"Gonna be a good time," Dickie agreed. "Go on, go on!" He had a stopwatch in his hand.

They flew down the stretch, passing other horses like an express train passing stations, and as the horse went under the wire Figaro slapped his stopwatch, and I brushed a finger on the surface of my phone.

My eyebrows went higher. 37.7 seconds. A ridiculously good time for three furlongs on this track. A bullet work.

"Oh *damn!*" said the heavy-set man, who had also been circumspectly timing the breeze. "Dickie, you got a live one there!"

Figaro laughed, looking triumphant. But he sighed after a moment. I knew why—he knew we'd buy the horse now, one way or another. Another lost stakes horse for Dick Figaro, claimer extraordinaire.

"Will you stay and see a few more go out?" he asked. "I have some live ones."

"I have a flight to catch," I said. "We'll be in touch."

"You could get on him in the shed," Figaro suggested suddenly. "You do the riding down there, is that right? I thought that's what someone told me. You're Alexander's foreman."

I paused. "That's right," I admitted. I was tempted by the thought of getting on the colt. I remembered the way Red Erin had felt beneath me, such an easy sway to his movement, and how I had been able to swing aboard and instantly sink down into him, past the leather of the saddle and the foam of the thick saddle-pad, and feel his muscles move my muscles, so that we danced in tandem.

And practically speaking, I had to see how the colt cooled out. I couldn't just leave. That had been a very fast work —almost too fast. What if he came in with a misstep? What if he'd strained something out there? I wanted nothing more than to gather up my things from the hotel and race back to the airport, but it was going to have to wait until work was over.

I went reluctantly out into the cold, and we picked our way across the hard, frozen ground, dodging horses and riders on their way out to the track, and back into the barn. "He'll be right back in," Figaro said. "There's a spare hard hat in the tack room. I'll just throw you on and you can give him a couple of turns, see how he feels to you."

"Okay," I said, ducking into the tack room. The walls were festooned with bridles, martingales, yokes, and a dozen different kinds of noseband. I saw the black hard hat and snatched it down, shaking it out for potential spiders and mice (skipping this step is a mistake you will make only once) and then putting it on right over my fleece cap. It was a snug fit, but it would be only be on for a few minutes. I could take it the squeeze, and heaven only knew who'd had this hat on last. I pulled off my coat, because I'd need some ability to twist my body, and slung it over a saddle, before heading back out in the shedrow.

The horse was there, coming around the corner, his head up, his ears pricked, his nostrils fluttering red. Figaro met him in the center of the barn and explained the situation; Marco nodded and hopped down. He took the reins and Figaro gestured for me to come and get a leg-up.

"Hurry, he's hot," he said, and I came down the aisle, set a knee in Figaro's cupped hands, and grasped mane and saddle. He pushed up with his arms, I pushed down with my arms, and then there I was in the little exercise saddle, just as I was every morning of my life, and I took the wet washy rubber reins in my hands as Figaro walked the horse forward again. He looked up at me. "Is it okay if I let him go?"

I nodded, sitting down deep in the saddle and taking the neckstrap of the yoke in my left hand, just as I did at home every morning, as an extra little security handle against unexpected spooks and bolts. The horses along the shedrow shook their heads and pinned their ears at us, the pigeons flew from the rafters in front of us, and I was riding The Tiger Prince around the Aqueduct shedrow as if I belonged there.

It was a funny thing, being on a horse in the city. To look out through the dirty windows and see the expressway a little way beyond. To hear the airplanes shrieking and roaring overhead, so loud that conversations paused with each interruption from above. To wake up in an apartment building and take a car through the dirty streets in riding boots, put on a hard hat and get on a horse. It couldn't have been any further from my green mornings in Ocala, with the air so fresh it ought to have been bottled, noisy only with whinnies and birdsong. And yet the horse felt the same. Horse between my legs, reins between my fingers, everything familiar and normal, just placed in this alien landscape, almost as if to confuse me, and only me, on purpose.

The feeling of sitting on Red Erin, feeling his same mannerisms and characteristics of gait, made it even stranger.

I gave him three turns of the barn and then Figaro came up to catch him. We went into his stall, me ducking my head to avoid rapping it on the top of the doorframe, and the trainer took the reins so that I could dismount and take off the saddle. We went through the ritual; I took the saddle over my arm, took the bridle over the horse's ears, dipped the bit in the water bucket to wash it clean of saliva and leftover hay, and went across the shedrow to the tack room to put it all away. Figaro grinned at me as he took the horse out and flung a cooler over his sweaty back. "Some things are the same no matter where you are, I'll bet!"

A hotwalker came up to take the horse, and off he went down the shedrow again. I watched him carefully, but everything was perfect. His movement stayed just as even as it had when he'd left the stall. A perfect machine, a lovely clone of his red brother. I had to have him.

Alexander would put him on the next truck headed south. I would send him a message the second I left.

"Can you call me a car, Dickie?" I asked. "That was wonderful, but there's something that I have to do."

Fourteen
Ask Parker

"I specifically requested the bay Thoroughbred that was used in the lesson last night," I said stubbornly, eyeing the chestnut Arab who was standing tacked up for me. The instructor squared her jaw and looked annoyed.

"We can only honor horse requests if they are placed with a little more notice," she said icily. "And if we are certain that your riding abilities are up to the challenge of the requested horse."

"Oh, please!" I snapped. I'd been up for more than thirty hours and I was in no mood to be polite. "I'm wearing riding boots and I stink of horse. I came straight here from Aqueduct—look, here's my receipt from the driver! I just got off of a racehorse, I have to go back to Florida to deal with my other two *hundred* horses, and it's just *really bloody important* that I ride this one Thoroughbred before I go back. So please do me a favor, charge me extra, do what you want, but send this pony back up and bring me what I want."

The riding instructor narrowed her eyes, but she did look me up and down, inspecting my worn paddock boots and the tell-tale dark stains on the inner seams of my jeans, where The Tiger Prince's sweat and hair had rubbed off during my brief ride. "We'll have to charge you," she said finally. "If you'll go back to the office, Diane will write it up for you. We'll have Parker down in a moment."

She took the Arab's reins and pulled him around, shaking her head. I went back into the little office and smiled congenially at Diane. "We're going to do a horse request," I said conversationally. "I would like to ride Parker. So if you'll just add that to my bill..."

"Without an evaluation lesson? Are you sure that's right?" Diane looked dubious. She pushed her hair behind her ears and thumbed through a lesson log. "I thought you said you'd never been here before."

I leaned on the desk. "Diane, I'm a professional trainer. I'm going to ride that half-broken-down Thoroughbred that was carting around some old novice like he was her personal bounce castle, okay? So please just let me pay you so that I can ride this horse and then make my flight?"

It's entirely possible that after spending a night out, an excessive amount of alcohol, and the ride at the racetrack, I was looking insane and dangerous. Whatever it was, Diane leaned back in her chair and nodded. I went back out into the arena to await my steed.

And then there he was, the darling boy I'd seen the night before. He stepped into the arena at the instructor's side, looked up at me, and pricked his ears delightfully. The instructor didn't waste a glance on him, just walked up and handed me the reins. "The mounting block is over there," she said, gesturing to a corner.

I led Parker over to the mounting block. I could mount from the ground with these long stirrups, but who needed to? His back wouldn't thank me. Although, in retrospect, the damage was already done to his back, and there probably wasn't much more I could do with one mount from the ground, not after all the years of riding lessons pounding up and down on him.

The dressage saddle felt good, like it was hugging my legs and seat, and I kicked away the stirrup irons so that I could sway with the horse and get to know him. The instructor kicked at a clod of dirt and looked bored. She'd already written me off as a rebel, not worth her time. Which was good, because all I really wanted to do was ask Parker a very important question.

I closed my knees tight against the saddle and rose out up into a very un-dressage-y pose, nudging Parker into a trot, and after a couple turns around the little arena, I pressed my hands into his neck, close to his withers, and clucked in his ears. He burst into a lively little canter, almost too big right away to be confined to the tiny space, and I laughed delightedly.

"What are you doing?" the instructor snapped. "Slow him down! You haven't warmed up!"

"Alright, alright," I conceded, sitting down in the saddle again, and Parker immediately tucked his chin in and came down to a springy walk. "Give me a riding lesson now, will you? I promise to behave."

On the way out, I picked up a card with the stable's phone number. If they were going to be closing, the horses would be for sale. Parker had answered my all-important question about where souls like ours belonged, and I intended to put *two* horses on that truck to Florida.

Fifteen
Finding the winner's circle

"He'll do fine, he'll do fine, he'll do fine." I was muttering under my breath, fully aware that I looked and sounded like a crazy person. There weren't that many people in the paddock, though, and the horses hadn't been brought around from the stabling yet, so the only person that caught my insane mumbling was Alexander. He quirked an elegant eyebrow at me.

"Are you going to be okay?"

I gulped and nodded. "I am in total control."

He nodded back, looking skeptical, but he stood a little closer and put his hand on the small of my back to draw me close. Far down at the clubhouse turn, at the other end of Tampa's little grandstand, the horses were emerging onto the track to be led up to the saddling paddock. We stood in the lawn of green grass between the walking ring and the covered stalls, awaiting The Tiger Prince. There was half an hour to the fourth race, and the beautiful bay, our darling after nearly a year at the farm, was leading the parade, his ears pricked and his head high, inspecting his new surroundings. His mane stood straight up in the stiff breeze off the Gulf of Mexico, giving him the look of an ancient warhorse. But I knew better. He was my baby, and I was going to kiss that sweet little white spot on his nose when he got to the paddock.

I'd kiss him for reassurance and for good luck. I'd kiss him to protect him, to be his patron saint, to be certain that nothing would touch him as he went winging around the oval here for the first time. I was keenly aware of all our lost loves. So was Alexander. But we couldn't help investing our hearts in this horse, as we had in Saltpeter and in Tiger's brother before him, as Alexander had in his gray mare. With everyone else, we were sensible, we were practical, we were cold. We thought with the head and not the heart, as Alexander had always preached.

But you can't always be sensible.

He came dancing into the paddock, all twirls and flourishes, like a startled bird on the verge of taking flight. We had schooled him here last week, the whole routine, loading up on the trailer at five a.m., driving him down I-75 in the ridiculous snowbird traffic that clogs Florida's roads in winter, tacking him up in a stall in one of the low green barns and letting the jockey gallop him on the oval. In the afternoon we'd had a groom walk him over in leg wraps and a white scrim sheet, walk around the paddock as if he was going to compete, letting him look at the half dozen horses entered in that race, and then took him back to the stable to chill for a while before loading him up for the trip home. He spent that night in his little paddock with Parker, as always. We wanted to add to his routine, not entirely alter it. Alexander wanted to run him from home as long as the Tampa meet was in session.

"He hates being indoors," Alexander had reasoned. "You have to work with a horse's quirks, not try to cram a square into a circle. If a horse wants to be turned out, for god's sake, turn him out."

And it had worked. The horse had been like a wild animal when he'd come off the truck last March, jumping off of the loading ramp before the handler could get him to walk down, getting loose and running around the training barn like a crazy thing before I caught him with a bucket of sweet feed and a cooing voice that he seemed to enjoy. We turned him out with Parker, the New York school horse, with whom he'd bonded deeply on the long truck ride to Ocala. They had special nickers for one another, and we would sit on our porch in the evenings and look down the hill to where the two grazed nose to nose. They were only separated for the mornings, when Tiger had to come in for the morning work and spent some time in his stall, so that he wasn't entirely dependent on freedom of movement and friendship. Parker was eating hay in the backside barn now; Tiger had come to understand that at work time, Parker stayed behind.

Getting a horse over quirks like that can take a long time, and Alexander had been in no hurry to race him, anyway. The summer race meeting at Calder came and went. "Too far," Alexander said. "I *could* ship him down the night before, but what's the rush? Tampa will be here soon enough, and it will be cooler. I'm tired of racing horses in the summer anyway."

And with that, he slowed down our work pace. The grueling summers, where we crammed our mornings with endless work, so that it was done before the afternoon thunderstorms brought an abrupt ending to outdoor chores, had always been a bad reward for getting through the sleepless nights and endless days of breeding season. "We've been working too hard," he said to me one morning in late May. We were slouched over coffee at the kitchen table, dreading going back outside, knowing that there were broodmares and their growing foals to check on, and two dozen yearlings to groom for the end-of-summer sales. "You're riding too many horses and you're exhausted. And I'm about fed up with training horses in this heat. Half of them aren't sweating anymore and the other half are close behind. Humidity's killing them."

"Horses are from Siberia," I agreed, regarding my empty coffee cup with regret. I got up to put another pot on. "They're not evolved for tropical climates."

"Neither are humans," he grumbled. "Certainly not this human."

"Evolved on the shores of the cold North Sea," I teased him. "Hell, I grew up here, and even I think it's too damn hot to work."

He slapped his hand on the table. "That's it, then!" he announced. "We're going to start taking summers a little easier."

And so we had. And it felt wonderful. How much unhappiness can be caused by just *working* too much, especially when you work with the person you love? We were spending time together, all the time, as a matter of fact, but we were working the whole time. Alexander turned out everyone for the month of June, split up the training barn grooms between the broodmares and the yearlings, who had to be handled and groomed everyday so that they could be transformed from sunburnt hoodlums into model citizens who would parade at the sales with style, and we took the whole damn month off.

The discontent of winter and the strange night in New York were fading from memory. I looked back at it from time to time with detachment and curiosity. How could I have been so silly? How could I have thought of anything but this life, here, with Alexander? And I admit, it was especially easy to be content as we vacationed through June, with quiet mornings watching the horses from the kitchen, relieved to be in the cool indoors and be excused for just a little while from the steamy air pressing down on us. It was especially easy to be content when we'd slip upstairs to sleep in the afternoon, letting the storms pound the house, happy not to be caught out in one of the barns, waiting the lightning out, as we so often had, in a feed room, slouched on a stack of sweet feed bags.

The rich Gulf coast sunsets became an evening ritual, when the thunderstorms were growling their way out to sea and the sunlight burst through just in time, coloring the sky in green and pink and purple, unexpected combinations which spread out over the vast Florida sky. Tired of pressing our noses against the window glass, we braved the mosquitoes and the steamy air to watch them from the porch, which looked out over the prospect of the farm, to the west. The front porch, like a lot of Florida porches, had been a neglected place, given over to the humidity and the creepy-crawlies, too strewn with leaves from the live oaks and a constantly perilous habitat for fire ants, black widow spiders, palmetto bugs, and all the other other charming denizens of Florida, which is basically a mini-version of Australia, the Land Where Everything Wants To Kill You, to ever appear inviting. After we spent two hours enthusiastically sweeping and scrubbing and killing everything that moved, Alexander declared it reclaimed from the wilds, and sat down on the unearthed porch swing, hauling me down with him.

And when we went back to work, then, it wasn't so bad. We took it a little easier. Alexander hired a couple of new grooms, so less work fell directly onto my shoulders. We went out to dinner instead of presiding over evening feeding and then falling upon whatever strange concoction had been left in our freezer. "Manage more, do less," he told me, and I did.

I rode tough horses less, too, cheerfully giving up the more dangerous and exhausting rides to the career exercise riders. In the morning he would tack up his pony, an aged Thoroughbred mare named Betsy, and I would tack up Parker (now called Parker the Pony), and we'd ride out to the track with the sets. From the vantage point of the ponies, we'd watch the horses train, and Alexander would point out everything I needed to look for as a trainer. I graduated, I was promoted. I made it from exercise rider to assistant trainer. I loved it.

"It's common sense," Alexander said to an acquaintance one night, as we sat at the Starbucks near the Ocala Breeders' Sales pavilion, spreading across a table with magazines and coffees in a glamourous display of non-agrarian lifestyle. "You and Hilda should really try to get out more, too. Give the grooms a little more responsibility and stop doing it all yourself. Join us here in the evening. We thought we were being so responsible by working so hard, and all we were doing was killing ourselves and getting more and more miserable."

The man had five hundred acres and a horse for every one of them. He nodded. "Hilda told me last week she felt like she was getting tired of horses. I didn't know what to say, because I kind of agreed with her."

I glanced up from my *New Yorker* and smiled at him. "Do it," I said.

I wasn't tired of horses anymore. And while I rode less, I still got on a few horses, to feel out someone's silliness or odd steps, most of the time. And, nearly always, The Tiger Prince.

And so summer passed, and the yearlings were sold and went away to make someone else crazy, and fall came and yearlings started to arrive in the training barn to be started, and horses came and horses went, and

Alexander and I went on running the farm together, content in each other's company.

Through it all, through the June rest and the early morning works and the evenings and nights spent outdoors with his friend, The Tiger Prince thrived. We watched him and worried over him, but nothing happened. He didn't buck a shin, he didn't pop a splint. He never colicked and he ate all his food and looked for more. His dark coat gleamed and fat round dapples spread across his flanks. He was fit and handsome and ready to race.

And so here he was, on a cool winter's afternoon, wheeling around the paddock. He nearly reared when the steward flipped up his upper lip to check the tattoo hidden there, confirming that he was the horse on the entry. I frowned, watching him act the fool with his groom. "He needs a lip chain," I said tightly. "Didn't you tell him to put in a lip chain?"

"Of course I did," Alexander said. "When was the last time Roberto did something he didn't feel was necessary? I suppose he thought the horse would be quiet because he was outside last night." He shook his head. "Will you take him or shall I?"

"I'll take him," I said, and marched across the grass in my dress and oxfords. I was dressed up for the occasion, a touch of class that Alexander had always insisted on, but I didn't wear heels to horse races, unlike some women I had seen. I never knew when I might have to take a horse and do some work.

"Get him in the stall," I hissed at Roberto as I came close. "You should have a lip chain on him!"

Roberto silently took the horse into the number six stall, walking him in a tight circle to turn him around to face the activity. I snatched the lead shank and flipped up his upper lip again, sliding the chain that had been over his nose down and pulling it across his gum. I pulled the lead taut so that the chain was firmly against the gum, pinned there on his lip. He looked at me and stood still. It was all the warning he needed. Lip chains look terrible, but they're really the ultimate positive reinforcement: if the horse leans back from it and feels pressure, all he has to do to relieve it is move back into the groom's hand.

The handler doesn't have to do a thing; the horse figures it out for himself. Nose chains aren't nearly as effective: you basically have to hurt a horse to get his attention. And while a horse has to be contained in an explosive atmosphere to keep him from hurting people, other horses, and himself, hurting him isn't the right way to do it.

"You stand," I said fiercely, and the horse eyeballed me and stood rigid.

The valet came up with the jockey's saddle and girths, and Alexander came up in his suit and tie to do the honors of saddling. A man on each side, they fastened the girth and the overgirth together, and then I took the horse out to the walking ring, near the track, to do a few little circles. The jockey arrived, wearing our silks of green and white diamonds, and Alexander and he settled for a little chat on the grass in the center of the walking ring.

Suddenly Alexander was beside me, hand out for the jockey, and while we walked the jockey set his knee in Alexander's hand and hopped into the saddle, taking up the reins, and nudging his feet into the tiny stirrups. Tiger put his head up and tried to trot sideways; I gave him a warning nudge with the chain. *"Don't,"* I said in my deep, oh-son-you're-in-trouble-now voice, and he settled down to a mincing, bouncing walk, hooves barely touching the mulch.

I had loosened the chain as we neared the track ponies, who were waiting in a little clump near the open gate from paddock to track, and as an outrider leaned down with his leather strap to slip it through Tiger's bit-ring, I popped up the buckle on the halter and dropped it from his head. For a second, it was just the jockey and the racehorse, but the horse didn't know it, and then the outrider was in control, taking them out for the post parade and a little pre-race warm-up.

Alexander was there beside me as they went dancing into the deep track, his hand on my shoulder. "He'll be fine," he said, and I could only nod. There went our boy. And I'd been so caught up in keeping him calm and together, I'd forgotten to give him his good-luck kiss.

Shrouded by oak trees, the chute at Tampa is nearly invisible from the grandstand. We stood by the rail at the finish line, watching on the screen as seven naughty two-year-olds were coaxed into the gate. The three horse reared and a collective *oh* came up from the little snowbird crowd as horseplayers fretted over their bets and spectators fretted over the horse. Then he was down, everyone was in, and then they were off.

The six hole was a tough spot for a speed horse like Tiger to make his first start; if he didn't break first, and no one expected him to since he was new to it all, then he'd have to sit back behind horses around the backstretch and he'd get dirt in his face, something that he had never experienced before. It was to be an afternoon of firsts, then. He broke slowly and his jockey settled him at the back of the pack.

"His ears are pinned," I said, worried, watching the feed on infield screen. "He's angry about the dirt."

"Or he's ready to give chase," Alexander said. "Watch. Jose will take him around the field at the turn and let him out at the top of the stretch. The track isn't favoring speed today. Not a single front-runner has won here in two days. And no matter what, he'll pick off a few, at least, and learn something."

I held my tongue and watched. I was here to learn. I was an assistant trainer now.

But that was my baby out there. I leaned against the chain link fence as they hit the top of the stretch. The front-runner was stretching out now. He didn't change leads and the jockey gave him a smack to remind him. Nothing. From behind the pack, Jose finally swung Tiger wide and showed him the empty track ahead.

"I want you *to win!*" I shouted, and Alexander clicked his tongue.

"It's really unlikely that he wins his first start, dear, you know that," he said, but he was a little breathless, and I knew neither of us were thinking with our heads now.

"Come on, *come on, come on!*" I shrieked, as Tiger's ears pricked, and he started to make his run. Without the dirt in his eyes, he was having fun. He picked off two horses, then three. There were three ahead still, two running in tight tandem, eye to eye, unable or unwilling to pull ahead of the other, as some young horses will do, relying on each other for solace in this new scary world of afternoons and shouting people. The frontrunner, close to the rail, flattened out suddenly, his race over a furlong too soon, and the two horses swept past him as if he were standing still. Behind, the pack of also-rans were forced to check as they caught up to the exhausted pacemaker. Tiger stayed wide, alone, running down the pair that would not be separated. A lone furlong left! Just a few jumps behind! Alexander slapped his hand on the fence, over and over and over, in cadence with the bobbing head of the dark colt.

He was startlingly close to us as he ran under the wire; he'd run so wide he was in the center of the track, but he'd done it, he'd caught the twins, and I could have sworn that he flicked an ear in our direction, and rolled a dark eye our way, as he passed by within earshot of our screams and whoops.

I was still jumping up and down, careless of the very real possibility that I'd flash the crowd (I wasn't really used to wearing skirts) when Alexander put a hand on my shoulder and said, "Now you save your celebration until he has walked soundly in the shedrow and you know he hasn't hurt himself." He peered down the track; the horses had pulled up and were jogging back to the finish line to be unsaddled and sponged off before their walk to the barns. "He looks good now, though."

"They're always work, aren't they?" I said, half-angry. "I can't just have a good time, and be happy with my horse, I always have to be watching and worrying. . ."

"The head and not the heart," he sighed. "But I do love that horse."

I smiled, watching him jog down in front the stands, shying at the bettors leaning over the fence, the children shouting for the jockey's attention. "I love him too."

about the author

After twenty years of working with countless horses in half-a-dozen disciplines, Natalie Keller Reinert packed away her saddle, put her feet up on the tack trunk, and started writing. From the short stirrup classes at dusty hunter/jumper shows in Florida to galloping over the inner dirt at Aqueduct Racetrack in New York City, it's always been about the Thoroughbreds, her favorite subject. Now settled in Brooklyn, New York, with her husband Cory and son Calvin, she pursues numerous literary projects, watches racing from the rail, and listens to way too many records.

You can stay in touch at:
http://www.nataliekreinert.com

Made in the USA
Middletown, DE
18 August 2017